PE
F
TALES

PERTHSHIRE
FOLK
TALES

LINDSEY GIBB AND
C.A. HOPE

The
History
Press

First published 2018

The History Press
The Mill, Brimscombe Port
Stroud, Gloucestershire, GL5 2QG
www.thehistorypress.co.uk

Text © Lindsey Gibb and C.A. Hope, 2018
Illustrations © Melissa Shaw, 2018

British Library Cataloguing in Publication Data.
A catalogue record for this book is available from the British Library.

ISBN 978 0 7509 8254 2

Typesetting and origination by The History Press
Printed in Great Britain

ABOUT THE AUTHORS

LINDSEY GIBB is a professional storyteller living in Highland Perthshire. She grew up surrounded by stories, and her love of nature and history is reflected in her storytelling. She performs all over Scotland as well as delivering workshops and enjoys collecting tales from her local area.

C.A. HOPE grew up in Scotland surrounded by books and history, where reading and writing were encouraged. She works in wildlife conservation but there is never a time when she is not absorbed in a writing project. Her enthusiasm for history drives her to bring the past alive by engaging and entertaining readers.

About the Illustrator

MELISSA SHAW is Scottish, living in Perthshire. She attended Stirling University, graduating with a BSc in Conservation Biology and Management (Hons). She has always enjoyed creating pieces of art, whether drawn or crafted from wire and beads. She is particularly inspired by wildlife, especially insects or imaginary magical creatures. Her enthusiasm for new experiences meant she was delighted to contribute to *Perthshire Folk Tales*.

CONTENTS

FOREWORD

Sitting between Scotland's highland line and her central belt, Perthshire has long been revered for her ancient stories. Carefully yet generously shared from one generation to the next, the inhabitants of Perthshire have opened doors into a world of ancient stories by protecting and nourishing both the history and tale that wraps itself around the times. In the past Perthshire spoke a form of ancient Gaelic, so no surprise to hear the mix of Scots and Gaelic tales intertwined in this book.

Tales from Celtic, Pict and all peoples in between remain as fresh today as they did all those centuries ago.

Perthshire is the seedbed of ancient tales and this book, with all its magical and mysterious tales, is a wonderful collection of many of those loved and handed-down stories.

Plucked from heather moorlands, stormy seas, deep mist -covered lochs, hidden lochans, sparkling waterfalls, concealed caves, bracken-strewn braesides, little black houses, mighty castles and many unseen places from Scotland's keeper of ancient tales, the authors have gathered a selection to please every lover of the 'tale'.

The authors have spared no inch of Perthshire as they searched nook and cranny unearthing gems awaiting lovers of myths, legends and historical stories concealed within the following pages.

Beginning their journey for the reader's delight they start in the south, opening the imagination with 'Golden Cradle of the Picts'.

The authors then lead us onwards sharing tales, which leap like the giant River Tay salmon, heading east with gems such as 'The King and the Fool', then travelling westwards onto a platform of wonder with 'The Cailleach of Glen Lyon', to finish the journey moving north with other magical stories such as 'The Witch and the Shepherd'.

If, during twilight hours, you wish nothing more than a few quiet minutes, draw the curtains, curl up with a comfy cushion and relish away the hours within the wonders of this book.

If the open spaces are to your liking then why not add this book to the flask and sandwiches as a worthy addition to the backpack. There are stories to suit any environment and atmosphere. Watch the children's wide-eyed wonder at the hidden gems in the pages of this excellent book.

In times gone by, at the end of the day, a long-awaited highlight of children's lives was always a story; tales of good witches and not so nice; tales of urisks and the wee broonie who did all the work no one would do during daylight; also faerie tales, giants and countless heroes and heroines, plus tales of tears and laughter and enchantment of ghostly goings-on.

Today we rely so much on electronic gadgets that we have forgotten that a simple telling of a story can open the mind of a child and raise them onto levels of creativity that helps in ways no man-made system can.

Perthshire Folk Tales can take readers, young and any age, to places they have seldom been, on flights of fancy and fantastic journeys where all things are possible!

I thoroughly enjoyed every story and can't wait to hear how you enjoy these droplets of gold awaiting your delightful immersion.

Note: It is believed that the Picts (painted ones) built Perth (Bertha), the city that sits on the River Tay, Perthshire's arterial lifeline for most of the source-beds to the fantastic tales in this book. Experts claim both Celt and Pict were amazing storytellers, so given the wealth of the ancient stories included here perhaps the authors may well hold a measure of both Pict and Celt in their veins.

To understand both the historical links and the old and ancient times of Scotland, the county of Perthshire holds all in the palm of her Pictish hands.

Jess Smith, 2018

A NOTE FROM THE AUTHORS

We are absolutely thrilled Jess Smith agreed to write the foreword for our book of *Perthshire Folk Tales*. Jess is an author, singer and award-winning traditional storyteller. She is one of the last of Scotland's Perthshire Travellers, well known for performing and telling her stories all over Scotland and beyond. Through her writing and storytelling, Jess keeps the old ways of the people of Scotland alive. Her mine of knowledge has been gleaned from tireless research, her own Traveller's background and a passion for sharing Scotland's rich heritage. Sincere thanks to you, Jess.

The beautiful illustrations accompanying the stories are the work of the very talented Melissa Shaw. We are so lucky that, despite her hectic schedule, Melissa embraced this project and remained unfazed by some of our stranger requests! Her skill and enthusiasm has created delightful drawings to complement the individual nature of the tales.

In our search through the abundance of Perthshire tales and legends, we are indebted to generations of Travellers, storytellers, ministers of the church and all the folk who told and retold these stories over the passing years. There is one young lady in particular who provided us with a veritable treasure trove: Lady Evelyn Stewart Murray.

Lady Evelyn was the youngest daughter of John Murray, 7th Duke of Atholl, and his wife Louisa. We shall be forever grateful to Lady Evelyn who, in her early twenties, undertook the mammoth task of travelling around the Atholl Estates writing down the folk tales and songs of her father's tenants. Originally recorded in Scottish Gaelic in 1891, they were translated by Sylvia Robertson and Tony Dilworth and published as *Tales from Highland Perthshire* in 2009.

The following tales are laid out roughly as if you are approaching Perthshire from the south, then heading east, across to the west and finally venturing into the north: Highland Perthshire. The general nature of the tales change as you move from the benign rolling hills and fertile land of the southern areas, up into the rugged, mountainous north. The borders of the county have been moved many times over the centuries and will, no doubt, move again, so as a rule of thumb we have included a story if it was set in Perthshire at the time it happened.

Whether tragic or funny, supernatural or magical, it has been a pleasure and privilege to retell these tales and keep the lives, beliefs and experiences of our ancestors resonating into the future.

LG – Thanks to my mum for sharing her love of stories and storytelling with me and to my fabulous friends for their support, particularly Cat, Dot, Shiona and Munro. The biggest thanks of all goes to Cherry, who made the book happen.

CAH – This was a very different writing venture for me! Many thanks to Lindsey for making this such an enjoyable collaboration.

MAP OF PERTHSHIRE

STARTING IN THE SOUTH

GOLDEN CRADLE OF THE PICTS

Over a thousand years ago the great country we now call Scotland was in the grip of power struggles between the Vikings, the Scots and the Picts. Stories handed down through generations provide a vivid picture of relentless violence. Bloody battles raged, driven by both intelligence and brawn, and the wily strategies to take control of the people and land became the stuff of legend.

One such tale has lasted the test of time and concerns the town of Abernethy in the middle years of the ninth century.

At dawn on a summer morning, King Drust of the Picts set out from his stronghold at the base of Castle Law with the last of his warriors. Years of fighting had reduced them to a motley force but they marched proudly behind their King, standards waving, their loved ones cheering and crying until they were out of sight.

King Drust knew his reign was coming to an end. He was heading north to Scone to face Kenneth Alpin (Cináed mac Ailpín), King of the Scots. There are two versions of the terrible events which occurred that day, and which one you believed depended on whether you were a Pict or a Scot.

Some say the Scots set a deadly trap for King Drust. The two enemies were meeting for an uneasy banquet at Scone where there was much revelry, music and dancing, with Kenneth's serving girls keeping the goblets well-filled with liquor. While the Picts were in a jovial, numbed state, the Scots made their move. Pulling out pegs from under the long trestle seats, they dropped their enemies into prepared trenches filled with blades and sharpened spikes.

The other version tells us King Drust led the charge against the King of the Scots on the battlefield and was cut down and killed amid the bluster and courage of the fight.

Either way, King Drust was killed.

Fleet-footed runners rushed south over hills and through glens to carry the tragic news back to the Pict's fort at Abernethy. Before leaving, King Drust had warned his wife and all the members of his household of the inevitable Scots' victory, so the news was not unexpected. They recalled his passionate words, urging them to make the best of their lives under the Scots rather than be needlessly slaughtered before their time.

Nevertheless, on hearing confirmation of his death, the fort erupted into wailing, cursing, arguing chaos. It would not be long before Kenneth's soldiers would be at the door to take their gold and quash any revival. The older folk believed they should stand firm: they were Picts until the day they died and would not submit to the Scots. Others felt it was futile and started to unbar the door, preparing to kneel before their victors and keep their heads on their shoulders.

Up in one of the attic rooms, King Drust's faithful old nursemaid scoured the horizon for any sight of approaching Scots. She was disgusted by the feeble cries of defeat and had a far more important subject on her mind. While the queen wept and wrung her hands downstairs in the main hall, the old nurse moved rapidly to take action.

Ever since he was born, when she cared for him as an infant, King Drust had trusted her implicitly. In recent years, he had made her responsible for the two most valuable things in his life and she knew these two things would be the first to be taken by the King of the Scots: his baby son and the cradle in which he lay.

The golden cradle was an ancient royal heirloom. Wrought from solid gold, nobody knew where it came from nor who created such a wondrous work of art, only that every baby born to a Pictish king was laid in this cradle. Oh, how much the King of the Scots would want to own this potent symbol of the Picts!

She knew what she must do. She knew she couldn't pick up the cradle. It was very, very, heavy and had remained as if stuck to the floor for many a year. There was no time to lose but she could barely even drag it across the floorboards so she ran down to the kitchens. Within minutes she was back in the attic with the baby's devoted young nursery maid and a brawny but brainless young man. They clustered around the golden cradle and managed to haul it down the back stairs, baby and all. Leaving the fort by a secret door, they scurried towards the cover of trees overhanging a burn and headed up Castle Law, staggering and slipping beneath their burden. Behind them came the terrifying sound of the approaching spear-wielding Scots, King Kenneth riding at the front.

The nursemaid may have been in advancing years but her heart and lungs were strong. All the way up Castle Law she muttered under her breath. Bullying and encouraging the servants to keep going, she vowed to stop the cradle and the infant king from falling into the Scots' hands.

When they reached a shoulder on the hill they paused for breath, looking down at the besieged fort. Below them, one of the Scots' soldiers noticed the sunshine glinting off the radiant gold and a cry went up! Kenneth's sharp eye recognised the cradle and he set off in pursuit with a group of soldiers.

By the time they came over the brow of the hill, the nursemaid had moved on towards a loch. It was here, at the lochside, that they found her: alone.

She was sitting waiting for them on a rock above the water. The ribbons on her cap neatly tied, her skirts arranged over her knees, bare feet dangling in mid-air and her arms locked around the golden cradle. It seemed to the watching Scots that she took a breath, or perhaps she was speaking, for her mouth gaped open and her eyes focused on them as she pitched forward and plunged into the water.

King Kenneth shouted urgently to his men to dive in and retrieve the precious golden cradle, adding as an after-thought for them to save the royal baby. Shields and armour were unstrapped, heavy boots hastily unlaced with shaking, exhausted fingers but in these few short moments the hot summer day grew dark. Black clouds appeared, swirling overhead to send raindrops pelting down, whipping the loch's surface into a white froth.

Up from the water rose a colossal wave, its crest falling in an endless waterfall to rise again and again, twisting into the shape of a bony, writhing old crone. Her watery cloak billowed out from around her shoulders and the raging gale swept back her straggling white hair to show jagged features and oversized, staring eyes. Deep, resonating sounds reverberated through the ground like thunder, but it wasn't thunder. Words spilled from the towering supernatural creature in a voice so low and so loud and so shocking they were hard to decipher; even King Kenneth dropped to his knees.

Her warning given, the old hag disappeared back into the depths, leaving the rain hammering down through an eerie silence. Terrified and defeated in their quest for the golden cradle, King Kenneth and his men made their way off the hill, not daring to look back.

And what of the heir to the Pict throne, King Drust's baby son? Did that fiercely loyal nursemaid really drown her little charge, as she wished King Kenneth to believe? Or, did she sacrifice herself to divert attention from the little maid slipping away over the hills with a baby in her arms? If so, the bloodline of our ancient Pictish kings is still alive: somewhere.

Tantalisingly, a long time ago, golden keys were found in a local stream:

> On the Dryburn Well, beneath a stane
> You'll find the key o' Cairnavain
> That will mak a' Scotland rich, ane by ane.

These keys are said to release the hoard of Pictish gold which was hastily and secretly buried between Castle Law and Cairnsvain on that fateful day.

The words spoken to King Kenneth and his soldiers by the old hag from the water gave clues of how to claim the cradle from the loch. The exact words have been lost from memory but are loosely recalled as meaning a man (or woman) should go alone to the lochan at dead of night. They must go round the loch nine times, encircling it with green lines and only then will they find the golden cradle.

For anyone thinking of trying to retrieve the golden cradle, a caution should be given. Although many have attempted this feat, none have succeeded and, more worryingly, many have either lost their wits or never been seen again.

Away with the Faeries

It was nearing the Winter Solstice and two young men went off to buy some whisky from a neighbour's secret still in the next glen. They made their purchase and passed a few words with their friend then set off home, a barrel slung between them. It was a frosty afternoon and with only an hour or so of daylight left they strode along, their breath foaming on the air.

On passing a hillock, one stopped, catching hold of his friend's arm and urging him to pause and listen. A beautiful melody came tinkling from over the rise in the heather. They laid down the whisky and crept cautiously up to the crest of the hill, the music growing louder with every step.

A crowd of faerie folk were dancing to the wondrous music, whirling each other around and beckoning to the men to join them. The harmonious tune made their hearts sing and their toes begin to tap but the older of the two was wary.

'Come away, we must be gettin' hame.'

His friend did not move, delighting in the magical sight of fantastically vibrant colour and merriment beneath the darkening sky. Wee folk were flitting here and there, lighting scores of lanterns and candles, jigging and laughing along with the sweet notes from pipes and fiddles.

Again the other man tried to persuade his friend to leave but without success, so he went home alone, bearing the barrel on his back. The villagers were very suspicious. Where was his friend? What had happened? They searched high and low and did not believe the story of the faerie gathering. Tempers ran high and the man was accused of killing his friend and hiding his body.

'I tell you the truth!' the man pleaded. 'I left him watching the faeries and he was alive and well. Allow me one year and I shall prove I am no murderer.'

Exactly a year since he last saw his friend, the accused man returned to the hillock. There, in the same place as he had left him, stood his friend!

'Come awa' hame now,' he told him.

The friend waved a hand impatiently, 'Och, man, let me watch. Just a minute or two more.'

'Ye've bin here a full year, come away hame noo!' He grasped his friend firmly by the jacket and after a struggle, he dragged him home. They argued all the way back along the track, with the rescued man flatly refusing to believe he had spent more than a few minutes watching the faeries. It was only when he reached his village and everyone ran out to see him, and his mother and wife both fell on him with tears of relief, that he began to doubt his own mind.

Then he saw the calf he left in the barn, now a stout beast, but on opening his front door he came fully to his senses. His son, a babe in arms when he left, came running across the parlour with hands outstretched to be picked up. He hugged the child close and declared that yes, he must have been away with the faeries for a full year.

St Serf and the Dragon

On the southern bank of the River Earn, a few miles south of Perth, lies the pretty village of Dunning. Nestled below the Ochil Hills, its perfect setting has been chosen as a safe, fertile dwelling place for at least the last five thousand years.

There must be many tales from Dunning from early Iron Age settlers and Roman camps but this story has been kept alive from when Scotland was Pictland.

Fifteen hundred years ago, the daily lives of the Dunning villagers revolved around raising families, rearing livestock and making sure there was plenty food for everyone.

One day, this happy existence was brought to a standstill when a dragon came marauding off the hills. It stamped its way towards Dunning's cluster of wooden houses, snatching up and eating small animals and whole fruit trees; dribbling and chomping as it went.

Mothers grabbed their children and fled indoors, barring the windows and doors. Men pushed their frightened live-stock into byres and guarded the doors, armed with sticks and pikes, terrified.

The beast swaggered across carefully tended vegetable patches, its tail swiping from side to side, knocking down haystacks and trampling woodpiles as if they were twigs. After several awful, breath-holding minutes, it stomped on across the floodplains and took a drink from the Earn. Then it returned to the hills and was lost from sight.

Of course, the appearance of a dragon caused a terri-ble uproar! Nobody felt safe and, worse, few people at the markets in Perth or Auchterarder would even believe it happened.

Unfortunately for the people of Dunning, the dragon kept returning.

There was a very holy man travelling through Strathearn, St Serf. He had held the office of Pope in Rome for seven years before finding it too restrictive and setting out on his own as a missionary. His footsteps took him up through Gaul (what we now call Europe) then across the Channel and northwards until he reached Pictland.

By this time, he had already founded a religious community on an island in Loch Lomond, now called St Serf's Inch. His restless, evangelical nature kept him moving, earnest in his duty of spreading the word of God and stamping out pagan beliefs. For all that, he was unanimously found to be a kindly, benevolent man by everyone who met him.

When St Serf drew close to Dunning, the villagers ran out to greet him. They invited him in to one of the elder's houses and told him of the 'dragon, great and loathsome, whose look no mortal could endure'. He listened, solemnly, while they ogled at this foreign holy man. With his aquiline features, dark eyes and black beard he was a fine sight, being the son of an Arabian Princess and the King of Canaan.

Suddenly a cry went up: 'Dragon!'

Everyone rushed about shouting, shooing chickens, banging doors shut, slamming bolts home and barricading themselves indoors.

St Serf went out to meet the creature.

The dragon's huge head swung round, its glistening, bloodshot eyeballs pointing directly at the approaching figure, straight-backed and calm with just his faith and a staff in his right hand to defend himself.

Peeping through the gaps in their shutters, the Dunning folk watched in fascination as St Serf kept walking directly towards the dragon. It reared up and thrashed its tail, snaking out its long neck to bring its scaly head down low towards the man. At every breath and roar, the grass flattened, leaves ripped from the trees and St Serf's robes whipped back against his body, but he didn't falter.

Raising his staff high, he brought it down on the dragon's head with a mighty thwack, right between the eyes! The beast collapsed to the ground.

Tentatively at first, then in crowds, people emerged from their hiding places and ran to give thanks to the holy man.

From then on, the spot where St Serf slew the dragon has been known as Dragon's Den. St Serf stayed for some time and a church bearing his name was built there in the twelfth century, which can still be seen today by all who wish to visit.

THE LEGEND OF LUNCARTY

Over one thousand years ago, near the little village of Luncarty, a ferocious battle took place between the Scots and invading Norsemen. The skirmishes and conflict between these two nations ran for over two hundred years but it is claimed the clash at Luncarty in AD 980 is particularly memorable. Not only did it dramatically change the life of a poor farmer but it gave Scotland its national flower.

In the closing decades of the tenth century, Kenneth II reigned over the Scots. He was at Stirling Castle when a rider brought the dreadful news that Danes had landed near Montrose. Survivors fleeing the invasion told of men, women and children being killed and dwellings torched as the Norsemen advanced through the countryside towards Scone; the royal centre of Scotland.

Alarmed, King Kenneth declared a promise of payment in land or money to anyone bringing him the head of a Dane. Then, although nearing his fiftieth year, he gathered his army and led them north to do battle.

Dusk was falling on the second day of the march when the king reached Luncarty, a hamlet on the west bank of the Tay, just upstream of Perth. They were greeted with the news that the Danes were settling close by for the night, so the Scots also set up camp and planned to attack at first light.

However, King Kenneth was not the only one being given information on their enemy.

It was still dark when the Norsemen rallied and began to creep across the open meadows towards the King's men. The first the Scots knew of approaching danger was a cry of agony from a Norseman pierced by a thistle. Alerted by the sound, the Scots were sent scrambling to their feet and seizing their swords just in time to face the warrior figures charging towards them through the grey dawn.

Caught unawares, Kenneth hastily ordered his men to the east and west, taking command of the central force himself. It was a violent, bloody battle; the screams of pain masked by the crash of blades and roaring bluster of foe on foe bellowing their vicious intent. Men fell in heaps from both sides, the dead and dying lying entwined on the crushed woodland floor and pastures.

The overwhelmed Scots began falling back and it soon became evident to the king that the Danes were winning.

A farmer by the name of Hay was tending a patch of land nearby and stopped to watch. With rising horror he saw his countrymen retreating. Shouting to his two strong sons to unhitch the oxen, they brandished parts of the yoke and plough as weapons and dashed towards the affray, hollering and bawling.

All three men were tall and rugged, with muscular bodies built from a lifetime of labouring on the land. With their features contorted with murderous intent, hair and beards straggling wildly as they ran, they appeared to both friend and foe to be the forerunners of fresh reinforcements.

'Help is on its way!' they yelled, tearing down the narrow track between two hills where the king's soldiers were being driven backwards. 'You must not give up! Fight on! Help is here!'

Seeing these new, strong allies made it easy to decide between dying with honour on the battlefield or running away to be slaughtered by the Danes snapping at their heels. Kenneth's troops rallied to Hay's cries. As one mass, the Scots surged forward again, slicing and hacking with renewed valour.

The tide was turned. The exhausted Danes believed they were facing a fresh, fortified army and lost heart, and soon the Scots were victorious.

King Kenneth realised how close he had come to losing this vital battle and acknowledged the heroes of the hour. Had it not been for the spiky Scottish thistle his soldiers would have been massacred in their sleep. Legend has it that this is how the thistle became Scotland's national flower.

The country was also deeply indebted to the brave farmer and the King summoned Hay to Scone to bestow his reward. He dispatched the royal falconer to climb nearby Kinnoull Hill and release a peregrine. Wherever the bird came to light would mark the extent of the land he would give to the

Hays. The peregrine flew east for six miles over the hills and glens of the Carse of Gowrie and this land, bordered by the Tay, became Errol. The King also raised the Hay family to nobility by giving them a crest, depicting a falcon and three shields: the three men being the shields of Scotland.

Traces of the legend lie all around Luncarty in Thistle Lane, Denmarkfield, Battleby and Redgorton, whose name

originates from the Gaelic *Roch Gorten*, field of red or field of blood. In the 1700s bones and Viking swords were discovered when Sandeman, the mill owner at Luncarty, cleared land for bleaching fields. Across the Tay to the east, in the Carse of Gowrie, visitors can see and touch the Falcon's Stone.

The Hay family became the Earls of Erroll and while modern historians have a different version of the creation of the Earldom, it seems the legend has been embraced by the Hays with the names Merlin and Peregrine among current family members.

JANET'S DREAM

When Janet was a wee lass she loved nothing more than looking after her younger brothers and sisters. She yearned for the day when she would have her own babies and all who knew her said what a fine mother she would make.

During her twentieth summer, Janet attended a ceilidh in a neighbouring village and met Lachlan. From the first moment of meeting, Janet knew she wanted to spend the rest of her life with this broad-shouldered young man with his shining blue eyes, infectious laugh and a love for dancing reels. Happily, Lachlan felt the same and they were married before the year was out.

The young couple settled into a loving married life but over the following decades Janet changed from a fresh-faced, smiling girl to a quiet, down-in-the-mouth woman. Her friends were having babies, even her younger sisters were having babies, and while Janet would be the first to offer help during their confinements and tirelessly care for their children, an empty sadness stole the sparkle from her eyes. She never fell with child.

Every day, she prayed to God for a baby. If it was a boy, she fervently promised to raise him to dedicate his life to the work of God.

One night she had a vivid dream. In it, she saw herself in a place and knew that if she drank from a particular spring where it rose from the hillside, she would have a son. As soon as she woke, with the dream still clear in her mind, she ran straight from the house. She recognised the images in the dream and knew exactly where the water sprang up near her house.

In the silvery pre-dawn twilight, Janet dropped to her knees among a patch of reeds on the marshy slope. Clear water trickled up from the earth between some half-submerged stones. She pressed her cupped hands down against the moss and gathered the water, thirstily gulping mouthful after mouthful. It trickled down her chin and soaked her nightgown but she didn't care, it tasted exquisite.

Nine months later, Janet welcomed her son into the world. The doom-mongers and gossiping old crones who warned of any child being born from such an aged mother being either disfigured or daft were proved wrong. From his first breath, the boy had lusty lungs and a strong body with a sharp brain to boot.

She had always been popular with her neighbours, and Janet's happiness radiated out to everyone, so her story has been passed around firesides for generations. She may have come to motherhood late but she poured all her maternal instincts into nurturing her son and worked hard to keep her promise to God.

Janet's charitable works and cheery character brought attention from all members of society. On hearing how much she enjoyed the annual harvest feast, the duke ordered she be given a dress each year to wear to the dance.

This tale has a truly happy ending because her son became the minister of Inchture in the Carse of Gowrie and Janet danced at the harvest ceilidh every year until she was over 100. She died after celebrating her 104th birthday and seeing her grandson also enter the clergy.

THE PIPER OF GLENDEVON

Early one evening in Glendevon, a mother waved goodbye to her strapping young son and watched until he turned the first corner out of sight.

The lad was a skilled piper and he was off to Dollar, a journey of about six miles. It was cloudy but the air was warm and, being summer, he was lightly dressed. He tucked his pipes under his arm and set a steady pace, admiring the views of the Ochil Hills around him. Just after crossing the Garchel, a stream running into the Queich Burn, he paused to look up at the low, round hill known locally as Maiden Castle.

This inconspicuous knoll was long believed to be the home of faeries but it sat before him in the gathering dusk as normal and still as the surrounding land. It was very quiet. Without the crunch-crunch of his boots on the path, the complete silence of the glen was only disturbed by the trickling stream and a gentle sigh of wind shivering through the grass.

He pressed on but had barely taken a dozen steps when loud music shattered the peace! Swinging round, he found the hill transformed into a mighty castle set upon a mound. Brilliant lights beamed from its many windows, flickering and flashing when indistinct figures passed behind the openings, dancing and swaying to the musical beat. The front door stood open, beckoning.

Unable to restrain himself, he retraced his steps to take a closer look. At that moment a troupe of faeries came running from the mound, seized him and took him into the castle.

An otherworldly scene greeted his eyes in a huge gilded hall. Under blazing candlelight, hundreds of people were dancing to the strains of a lively band of fiddlers. With whoops of delight, the mass of whirling dancers flew round and round the floor, the ladies' gowns shimmering like rainbow-coloured butterflies' wings.

The faeries wanted him to play for them, so he primed his pipes, filled his lungs and began to play. Each piece of music ran into the next and the more he played the more they urged him to play again. For two days he piped and neither he nor the dancers grew tired. However, he became anxious about his family because he knew they would be very worried by his absence. The faeries gave their promise that they would let him go if he played a special dance for them but he must play it to their complete satisfaction. Knowing the tune, he threw himself into producing the best rendition he could produce of the very fast piece of music. Finally, on reaching the last note, the faeries burst into applause.

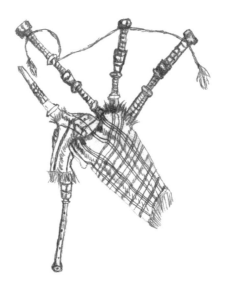

At last he was allowed to go and in an instant he found himself out on the hillside beside the Garchel. The castle was nowhere to be seen. The round hill was just a round hill, unremarkable in the gloaming. There was no sound except the wind sighing among the grass and the wee burn gurgling down towards the Queich.

The piper did not continue his walk to Dollar; instead, he jumped over the burn and hurried back to his home in Glendevon. He wished to allay their fears for his disappearance over the last two days but, bursting through his parents' door, he found the parlour filled with strangers.

They stared at him, asking what he wanted and who he was. He protested that this was his father's house and he had only been away a couple of days – what was more, where was his family?

They looked at him askance, noting the pipes under his arm and murmuring to one another. Then one of the women reached over and tapped the arm of an elderly man seated by the fire, waking him from his nap.

The man's rheumy eyes scrutinised the young piper for a long time before he spoke.

He said he remembered a time, seventy or more years ago, when he was a lad. His father told him a tale about a piper from this village of Glendevon who went away on a calm summer evening to pipe in Dollar. He had never been seen again. Despite years of searching by his family and friends, no trace of him was ever found.

The piper had been with the faeries in Maiden Castle for a hundred years.

THE KING O' THE BURDS

A wee wren landed on a tree beside an eagle.

'I am the biggest burd in the whole land,' proclaimed the eagle, stretching his mighty wings to their fullest extent and flapping them proudly. 'I must be the King o' the Burds.'

'Well now,' the wren said sweetly, hopping along the branch, 'I may be one of the smallest burds in the whole country but I do not believe the size of our wings has much to do with whether we are King or not.'

The eagle's head jerked round, turning the full attention of his yellow eyes to study the tiny brown bird. 'Why do you say that, wren?' he asked, looking imperiously down his huge hooked beak.

'Burds are set apart from all the other creatures by flying. Surely it is the burd who can fly the highest who is the King o' the Burds?'

'Ah, yes, you make a good point, wren,' the eagle relaxed, confident in his abilities. 'Come then, let's see which of us is King?'

They both swooped off the tree. The wren beat its wings furiously and flew straight up into the sky. The heavy eagle flapped its mighty wings and circled round and round, rising higher and higher, but still the wren was above him.

They flew for some time until the wren grew tired and landed lightly on the eagle's back.

When the eagle grew tired he spread his wings and drifted down, calling, 'Where are you wren?'

'I am above you,' replied the wren.

So, the wren became the King o' the Burds.

THE WIZARD

The vagaries of Scottish weather meant precious dry days suitable for harvesting were eagerly awaited in the fertile fields of Perthshire. When the crop was ripe and a fine day dawned, everyone pulled together to gather it in.

On one such September day, a farmer drove his horse and cart up to the edge of his corn to meet his willing neighbours. The sweet scented dew soon lifted in the morning sun and the men spread out and set to work with their scythes. Behind them, the womenfolk sang and gossiped while gathering and stooking the sheaves, the children running hither and thither gleaning any fallen stalks. It was thirsty work and the farmer's wife brought up flagons of weak ale and water, placing them in the shade beneath a hedgerow before hurrying home to prepare their midday meal.

With everyone reaping the harvest, she was alone in the house, bustling from store cupboard to larder, fireside to table, scrubbing, chopping and stirring. It was when she was shelling a score of boiled eggs that a knock sounded on the door and a tall, well-dressed gentleman stepped over the threshold.

He removed his hat politely and asked for a drink of milk. The farmer's wife barely looked up, telling him she only had a little milk and was saving it for the reapers.

He then asked for a drink of water.

She frowned and sighed, all the time cracking eggs against her bowl and skilfully peeling away the shells.

'There's no water in the house,' she said brusquely, 'can you no' see I'm busy on this harvesting day? I've far too much to do to trail down to the well an' draw some water for you.'

The traveller stood watching her for a few moments and then left, closing the door behind him.

He was no ordinary gentleman, this was MacDonald of Keppoch, a renowned wizard. Before leaving the farm he cast a spell on her and she started to dance.

The blazing sun rose to its highest point in the sky and the reapers drained the last drops from the flagons. Every few minutes they wiped their brows on their sleeves and glanced hopefully towards the house, expecting to be called to the feast. The farmer grew weary of waiting and sent one of the women to find out when the food would be ready. The woman did not return so he sent another. She did not return.

Laying his scythe on the cart, the farmer marched down to his house and looked through the window. His wife and the other women were dancing and jigging around the kitchen, unable to stop their feet from their merry steps. Sensing witchcraft at work he dared not enter, so he shouted to his wife, asking if anyone had called at the house.

'Yes, a gentleman asking for a drink,' she called back breathlessly, 'but he has gone on his way in the direction of Blairgowrie.'

The farmer ran to the barn and saddled his horse to gallop off after the traveller. He found the gentleman soon enough and demanded to know why he left his wife and the other women in such a state, adding indignantly that he was just a poor farmer in the midst of reaping his harvest and he needed MacDonald to return with him to set matters back to normal.

The wizard was in a hurry to reach his appointment in town and would not return to the farm, but he took pity on the sweating, red-faced farmer.

'Go back and look above the lintel of your door,' he said. 'There you'll find a small stick. Remove the stick and they will be relieved, the spell will lift. Oh, and tell your wife to be less unfriendly to travellers on the road in the future.'

The exploits of MacDonald of Keppoch feature in many a tale told beside campfires and hearths throughout Perthshire: here is another one ...

THE PACKMAN

On hearing a packman was in his house peddling his wares to the cook, MacDonald went through to the kitchen to speak with him.

'You journey far and wide for your business, tell me what news do you have?' he asked.

'I have no news, sir,' the young man replied, pulling his cap from his head and twisting it nervously with both hands.

'Goodness, man! Each day you must meet new people and hear the chatter from bustling parlours and markets. Surely there is something you have come across which I would like to hear?'

The packman shook his head and said he could think of nothing of interest to relate.

MacDonald clapped him on the shoulder, 'Ah well, the darkness is nearly upon us, stay the night here and you can be on your way in the morning.'

Before returning to his pipe and a dram by the fire, MacDonald instructed a maid to take clean linen upstairs and prepare the bedroom next to his own for their visitor. Pleased to be given shelter in such a comfortable and well-appointed house, the packman quickly made himself at home. He was no sooner undressed and snuggling down into the soft, aired mattress than he heard his host call out to him.

'Bring me a drink of water, I have a terrible thirst.'

Obediently, the packman jumped out from between the sheets and, pulling his long, thin undershirt over his head, looked around for a pitcher of water. There was none in the bedroom so he went downstairs only to find all the rooms empty and in darkness, the candles having already been snuffed out. He poked around in the unfamiliar kitchen and scullery but could not find a drop of water in the house. For a moment he was in a quandary, then a thought occurred to him and, keen to carry out the gentleman's request, he took a jug from the dresser and went outside.

He remembered having seen a river running close to the house so, despite being barefoot with his shirt hanging loose to his knees, he tiptoed down to the water's edge. It was difficult to gather water without disturbing the sandy shore and soiling the contents, so he stepped into the shallows. It was little better, with weed and flecks of dirt spoiling each filling. He waded further and further out until, at last, the jug was full to the brim with clear water.

His mission complete, he tried to return to the bank but the river was rising all around him, pressing on his legs and threatening to knock him off balance as his toes slipped on smooth, slimy rocks. It was suddenly bitterly cold and hailstones splattered into the water, pelting him through the thin cotton.

He was panicking and struggling to grasp a hold of an overhanging willow bough when a group of four men came into view. They were moaning and tearful, bent low beneath a burden they carried between them. To his rising unease, the shivering packman saw they were carrying a corpse.

'I cannae go on,' one man groaned, 'not another step.'

Another looked around him in despair then pointed to the man huddled under the willow. 'Look there! I recognise him as a packman I saw on the road. He is used to shouldering a heavy load. Come, we will put the body on the packman's back.'

'No you will not!' shouted the poor, bedraggled young man, but they dragged him from the water and put the corpse on his back.

The macabre little group walked on for more than a mile until they came to a churchyard, where the four men immediately began digging a grave.

'It is a deep hole, but is it deep enough?' one man enquired of his friends.

'It is hard to say. We will put the packman in the hole and then we can see if we need to dig further.'

'No, no!' the packman cried, exhausted. 'I shall not go into the grave!'

'Oh yes you will,' they muttered through gritted teeth.

His pathetic attempts to fend them off were to no avail and he was pushed into the grave. Shovelfuls of earth showered upon him yet the more he brushed them away and strived to scramble free, the thicker the soil built up over his body, pinning him down.

Summoning all his might to save himself from choking, he lifted his elbows and pushed the weight away, kicking with his legs at blankets and throwing himself around in a mass of bedclothes … on his bed.

The next morning the young man tried to leave the house before anyone stirred but was met by MacDonald in the hallway, who enquired how he slept.

'It doesn't matter how well I slept,' the hollow-eyed pedlar replied. 'I'll be going now and not troubling you again.'

MacDonald looked him up and down, a wry smile in his eyes. 'No, I dare say it does not matter, but when you arrived in my house you had no news for me, whereas you will have news to share wherever you go tonight!'

BESSIE AND MARY, TWA BONNIE LASSIES

It is easy to believe the Great Plague of 1666 was confined to
London but, the truth be told, it spread its evil far and wide.
Having smouldered in society since the Middle Ages it esca-
lated for ten years before the Great Fire cleansed the capital
city. Killing more than 200,000 people, bubonic plague
reared its head right across England and Wales. Despite the
Scottish border being closed and fairs cancelled, the dreaded
illness crept up into Scotland.

In the summer of 1666 there was an outbreak
of this vile disease in Perth which rapidly spread to
epidemic proportions.

It was not long before news of the rising death toll reached
the area of Lynedoch, four miles north of the city. On that
day, young Bessie Bell, the daughter of the Laird of Kinnaird,
was visiting her friend, Mary Gray. Mary's father was the
Laird of Lynedoch so, due to their fathers being acquaint-
ances and close neighbours, the two young girls spent most
of their childhood together and were very close friends.

On hearing that the plague was raging through Perth,
they decided to keep well away from the possibility of contagion and immediately sought out a place to hide. The pretty
rolling hills, woodlands and streams around Lynedoch were
bathed in summer sunshine, offering several inviting places
to shelter with a supply of fresh water at their side.

They chose the perfect spot under some trees beside the
Brauchie Burn at Burnbraes. It lay about three quarters of
a mile west of Mary's home of Lynedoch and they set about
building a bower to keep them dry. A plaited roof of elder
stalks was soon decorated with slim, leafy boughs of bird
cherry, hazel, heather and rushes. Then they gathered sweet
scented grasses, flowers and Lady's Bedstraw and covered it

with their cloaks to make a soft
mattress. While they went
about their craft, discuss-
ing the best way to tie
this or wind that, they
would sometimes share
a laugh before remem-
bering the frightening
reason for their bower and
would hug each other tight
for reassurance.

From their earliest years, Bessie and
Mary were bonnie wee lassies and when they grew up they
blossomed into strikingly beautiful young ladies. Naturally,
this attracted the admiration of all the local men but none
more so than a young man from Perth.

He adored the way Mary's golden curls swung and gleamed
when she walked and delighted in her quick wit and winsome
smile. However, he was also smitten by Bessie's bewitching
dark lashed eyes, the dimples in her rosy cheeks and her kind,
friendly nature. It was not long before he fell head over heels in
love with them both.

Mary and Bessie's friendship remained strong and true,
allowing his romantic behaviour to cause neither upset nor
jealousy between them.

It had become customary for this young man to call on
his sweethearts every few days and when he reached Bessie's
home at Kinnaird and was told she was not there, he became
concerned. He walked on to Mary's house, hoping the girls
were not unwell. A servant informed him the girls were safe,
keeping themselves away from the plague by living in the
open air beside a stream until the danger passed.

It did not take him long to find them and after assuring himself of their good health and spirits, apart from pangs of hunger, he promised to return with a supply of food. One day, after several weeks of this arrangement, he did not appear.

By the fourth day, when dusk leeched the colours from the landscape into hues of grey, the girls gave up their watch for his approaching figure and curled up together under their bower. Hungry and growing weary of their exile, they fell into a fitful sleep.

What they did not know was that their admirer had succumbed to the disease and died. Tragically, through his well meant visits and offerings, he had also carried the bubonic plague to his loved ones.

Whether Bessie and Mary knew their fate and attempted to nurse each other or if the end came mercifully quickly could not be told. Their poor, still, pestilence-ridden bodies were found side by side beneath the bower.

Due to the fear of contagion they were not buried in the churchyard but in a lonely place on the Burn Braes by the River Almond. Their gravestone can still be seen, inscribed: 'they lived, they loved, they died' and a ballad was written in commemoration of their short lives.:

Bessie Bell and Mary Gray
They were twa bonnie lassies
They biggit a bower on yon burnside
And theekit it ower wi' rashes
They theekit it ower wi' rashes green
They theekit it ower wi' heather
But the pest came from burrows toun
And slew them baith th'gither.

THE WITCH AND THE BRIDLE

Euan was the newest member of the Laird's outdoor servants and caused quite a stir among all the local lasses, including the lady of the castle.

Standing over six foot tall, he was a well-muscled, biddable young man who would happily carry out the hardest jobs on the estate. Whether scything hay, dredging the mill lade or digging out the midden, he could be counted on to meet each task with a smile and a nod of the head.

A few weeks after arriving, he woke up feeling as exhausted as when he went to sleep. In fact, he told Bobby, with whom he shared a mattress, he felt even more tired than when he lay down eight hours earlier. He struggled through the day smothering yawns and longing for the sun to sink below the horizon so he could take the weight off his aching feet.

In the middle of the night, a woman came to the side of Euan's bed. She whispered in his ear, he sat up, and she led him outside where she slipped a bridle over his head.

Immediately, he changed into a horse and she climbed astride, making him gallop for hours until they reached a brightly lit tavern in France. She left him tethered to a railing beside another horse before disappearing inside to drink and carouse with a group of witches amid wild laughter and music.

Just before dawn she came out, so intoxicated she had to make several attempts before succeeding in mounting him. With heavy hands, she wrenched his head around, jabbing the bit in his mouth and spurring him on furiously to return to Scotland. She jumped off him at the barn door, removing the bridle and sending him to lie down.

When the cockerel crowed and the servants woke to start the day, poor Euan could barely open his eyes.

Bobby patted him on the shoulder, 'I'll sleep on yer side o' the mattress the nicht an' Ah wager ye'll ha'e a better sleep.'

That night, the witch crept in as usual and bent over the bed, murmuring her spell. Bobby was not asleep, he had stayed awake, waiting for her to come. Sure enough, as soon as she put the bridle over his head he too changed into a horse and was ridden hard and fast over the dark countryside to France. This time, when she tied him up outside the inn, Bobby had kept enough of his senses to rub his head against the railing and soon he was free of the bridle.

When the witch returned, drunk and unsteady, he caught her unawares. Throwing the bridle over her head he blurted out the words of her own spell. In a flash, she turned into a beautiful golden mare with a flowing mane and tail the colour of whipped cream. He jumped on her back and made her gallop home but she was not as fast as Euan and Bobby and the dawn was already breaking. Seeing people were waking up, Bobby put her into the stables and hurried towards the barn to join the other servants.

'Bobby!' the Laird shouted across the yard. 'Come here, lad! I saw you ride in on a pure-bred mare, where did you get her?'

'Frae a friend,' Bobby replied, meeting his eye. 'She's a crackin' beast, if ye want her, ye can ha'e her.'

The Laird was delighted and they went to the stable and looked the horse over together before agreeing on a fair price.

'I see she's not shod,' the Laird remarked. 'Be a good fellow and take her up to the blacksmith and have him put some shoes on her.'

It was late afternoon before Bobby came back with the mare and the Laird was impatient to ride her. He took her for a canter down to the riverside and popped her over hedges and gates on the way back. Well pleased, he dismounted and led her into the stable, reaching up to remove the bridle.

From two fields away, Bobby and Euan heard his screams of distress.

As soon as he pulled the bridle over the mare's ears, she transformed into a willowy young woman with tousled blonde hair. Her hands and feet were dripping with blood but it was not only the gore which shocked the Laird.

This bedraggled, bleeding girl was the lady of the castle, his wife.

HEADING EAST

MESSY MORAG

There was a young shepherdess who lived high up on the hills near Pitmiddle. She was an excellent shepherdess, mindful of her flock and duties, they were well cared for and not one lost. Everything was well kept and managed. That is, until her cottage was reached.

She was so messy, sometimes just getting in the door was a struggle. She couldn't walk around the room without treading carefully, often things crunching under foot. Her mother despaired; how would she find a husband if she couldn't keep his house?

Morag wasnae worried, she wasnae in any hurry tae get married. Her friends would occasionally visit and offer to help tidy up but they were always politely and firmly turned down. Everyone, it seemed to Morag, was obsessed with tidiness; she was who she was.

As with all those that shepherd, she had a working sheepdog to help with the sheep. A streak of black and white across the hill, Fly was well suited to her name. And she had a cat to help keep the inevitable vermin down, a huge tabby-striped

cat, that probably had wildcat in its ances-
try. The cat was called Cat, as Morag
mused there was little point
naming an animal that paid no
attention to its name.

Cat and Fly did not get on.
No coorieing up together
on cold nights, no playful
chases at the end of the
working day and cer-
tainly no sharing of
food. They came to
an understanding where
they simply pretended the other didn't exist and this seemed to
work well, keeping peace and harmony in the untidy cottage.

One day Morag returned earlier than expected from
some errands in the nearby village and, as she came round
the corner of the cottage, she stopped in surprise. There,
sitting side by side, were Fly and Cat – most unusual, but
as she stopped to wonder, she realised they were not alone.
They appeared to be talking to a broonie, a small, wiry, hairy
creature. Morag's eyes got even bigger as all three headed
into the cottage. From where she was standing she could see
right inside.

The broonie walked forward and surveyed the room,
turned to Fly and Cat and shook his head before leaving.
The dog and cat looked at each other then headed their separate ways. Curious, thought Morag, and she watched them
both more closely than normal. The next day something
similar happened, she rounded the corner of the cottage –
having been tending to a sick sheep – and there was Cat and
Fly with another broonie, a taller, bulkier one smoking its
small pipe.

Once again the three went into the cottage and Morag watched as the broonie walked round the room, as such as it could, puffing furiously on its pipe. Then with a long, inward breath, sooking air between its teeth, it slowly shook its head. Once again, all three left.

'What on earth is going on?' thought Morag. She watched Cat bat some of the debris on the floor and Fly nose around, pushing it away. Suddenly she realised – they were interviewing broonies to come and clean her cottage!

The following day, Morag made a point of being elsewhere on the land on her own so she could quietly return and see what was happening. Once again, Cat and Fly were sitting together, this time talking to a smaller, much hairier broonie; it must be a female broonie as they are much hairier than the males. But this broonie wasn't standing still like the others; she was buzzing around brushing tangles out of Fly's coat and removing burrs from Cat's tail. Then they stepped into the cottage and the broonie turned to Cat and Fly with her eyes gleaming.

She leapt into the air and became a spinning blur, a blur that started to move round the room tidying and cleaning as it went. Soon, each part of the room would appear sparkling and spotless. But as the broonie blur moved to the final quarter of the room, the spinning began to slow down. It took longer for a section of the room to appear until, finally, there was just one corner left to do. But the spinning stopped, the broonie was on her knees and staggered to her feet before shaking her head at Cat and Fly and weaving an unsteady path out the door.

Well, from that day, Morag was a lot tidier. Oh, she would never be immaculate but at least she could walk around her cottage without tripping over things and people would visit without offering to clear up. But she left that one corner as it was, the one that defeated the broonie, and occasionally added to it, and it became known as 'the broonie corner'.

Broonie corners can still be found in many houses, if you know where to look.

THE KING AND THE FOOL

Back in 1406, the first King James took the throne of Scotland. James being a fine and noble name, a King James ruled until 1625, apart, of course, from the turbulent twenty-five years of Mary Queen of Scots. The following story is said to have taken place during the reign of a King James, providing a period of over two hundred years to choose from!

A priest was going about his parish work one day when soldiers came to his town. They stopped him on the road and issued a warrant from the King. An action or sermon made by the priest had reached the King's ear and greatly angered him. The nature of the crime has been lost in the mists of time but it caused a terrible reaction at the palace, culminating in calls for the preacher's execution.

The royal order summoned the priest to travel immediately to Scone Palace, the royal seat of Scotland. He must appear before the court where the King would pose three questions to him and if he could not answer them all correctly, he would be killed.

The priest requested leave from the soldiers to be allowed to call in at his home to change from the soiled smock he was wearing into his formal religious robe, more fitting for a royal audience. His real reason for returning to his house was to say goodbye to his brother, a simple-minded man known locally as the Fool.

'I am grieved to leave, there is much to tend to here and I would not choose to abandon you this way, brother. Do you understand?' The priest took him by the shoulders and looked affectionately into his eyes. With only three years between them and both taking their looks from their father, the two men were very similar. However, intellectually, the priest was a highly regarded scholar and the Fool was, well, he was a fool. His brother's welfare was of deep concern to the priest. Ever since their parents died he had provided him with shelter, food, sibling love and spiritual guidance. How would his daftie brother manage on his own? The few coins he earned from mucking out byres or clearing stones would barely feed him.

'You may stay in this house as long as the church allows,' the priest assured him. 'May the Lord protect you and have mercy on you. When I am gone I am sure our good neighbours will gather round and help you through life.'

'Wait,' said the Fool, snatching his brother's clerical gown from him and pulling it over his own head. 'I cannot let you go to your death. I shall take your place and when they kill me it will make little difference to the world.'

The priest protested forcefully but with his escort of soldiers waiting within earshot at the door, there was no time to reason with his dim-witted brother. Within moments, the Fool was dressed from head to toe in the balloon-sleeved cassock with his cap in place. In an uncustomary show of feeling, they embraced before parting. The priest moved stealthily to the window, his lips moving in an urgent prayer as he watched the soldiers marching away with his brother under their guard.

After many hours of travelling along the well-worn path to Perth, they crossed the Tay in a boat and marched up through green pastures dotted with oaks and elms to where Scone Palace stood.

On entering, he was held in a small room and offered bread and water which he accepted gratefully, believing them to be his last meal. Then he was taken to a grand hall, filled with the great and good of Scotland.

The deafening chatter of voices echoed up into the ornately plastered ceiling, rising to a crescendo when he was led through the doorway. All eyes sought to catch a glimpse of the priest who had so enraged the King. They pressed around him, ladies pushing as roughly as the men to take a closer look until the soldiers were forced to clear a way through the crowd to deliver their charge to the furthest end of the room. They left him there, standing alone, in front of a row of velvet-covered seats surrounding the throne.

Trumpets sounded and a hush fell on the company. Those seated rose to their feet, the men sweeping off their caps and bowing, the ladies curtseying low. The King entered.

Flanked by his court officials, King James took his seat on the throne and assessed the man standing before him.

'I shall ask you three questions and should your answers fail to satisfy me, you shall be killed.'

The Fool nodded and held his monarch's steely gaze.

'Tell me … where is the centre of the earth?'

A sycophantic murmur of amusement rumbled round the courtiers and the King arched his dark brows in expectation.

The Fool stamped his foot on the floor, 'Right here,' he replied.

Heads turned, questioning looks darted between the King and his advisors, the crowd shuffled uncomfortably.

'Well,' the King said at last. 'As the earth is round … I must concede your answer is correct.' He narrowed his eyes, the jewelled rings on his fingers sparkling as he stroked his chin. 'My second question. You see me before you, I am your King. What am I worth in money?'

'You can be worth no more than thirty pieces of silver, for the greatest man who was ever born was sold for that amount.'

A collective gasp escaped from the crowd.

'Aha!' the King leaned back abruptly against the carved oak of his throne. 'A good answer and one with which I find I cannot quibble.' He waited until the shocked assembly grew quiet again before posing the third and final question.

'Tell me … and this is much more difficult. Do you know anything which I am thinking about *right at this moment* but of which I am entirely wrong?'

Without a moment's hesitation the Fool said, 'Yes, you believe you are speaking to the priest but I am his brother, the Fool.'

The King jumped to his feet. Astounded, he cried, 'Good God! You are free, go home! If you are the Fool, your brother must be a very clever man indeed … and he deserves to live!'

The Harper's Stone (Clach a' Chlarsair)

A man from Atholl set out over the moors to Strathardle carrying his clarsach to play at a ceilidh. It was a bitterly cold day with several inches of snow on the ground and he was making slow progress. From time to time he came across a large stone among the heather, brushed off the snow and sat down to breathe some warmth into his chilled hands.

It was on one of these rests that he first noticed movement up on the hills to his left. Red deer? They must be searching the lower slopes for food in this harsh weather. Although the sun was masked behind cloud, he squinted at the glaring scene, scanning the grey and white landscape where waving grasses, shrubs and clusters of windswept trees had shed their white covering. There was little to see except a few birds and rabbits. Lifting his harp again, he walked on, picking his way.

The movement caught his eye again. This time it was right ahead.

It was a pack of wolves. Paralysed with terror, the man did not know what to do. The wolves would be hungry and he had no weapon to protect himself from becoming their meal. Feeling very vulnerable, he watched the powerful grey animals trotting straight towards him, their long backs rising and falling at every stride, tongues lolling, eyes fixed on their prey: him.

When they were within a few yards, the man impulsively looked for a large stone where he sat down and started to play. His hopes of scaring the wild beasts away were dashed. Instead of running off, they crowded together in front of him in a half circle. He played louder, reaching the highest and lowest notes he could muster with his freezing fingers slipping and plucking at the strings.

The largest wolf, the leader of the pack, took several steps closer, his moist black nose raised to sniff the air, ears pricking. The poor harpist was panicking. He did not know whether to look into its pale eyes or keep his head bowed but the animal's intense stare forced him to meet its gaze.

Then it stretched out a front leg towards him and he saw its paw was swollen. He stopped playing to take a closer look. A long blackthorn barb protruded from the footpad and, hoping it would not make matters worse, he pulled it out, bracing himself for what was to come.

The wolf swung away, paused to lick the paw for a few moments then pushed through the pack with a whining, growling noise deep in its throat. Giving the man a final glance, all the other wolves moved swiftly away, following their leader loping towards the hills.

Enormously relieved, the man went on his way with a spring in his step. He was eager to tell all his friends and family about his remarkable escape from almost certain death while alone on the moor with wolves.

A few years later the harpist was in a local market-place assessing the merits of acquiring new boots, when a well-dressed gentleman came up to him and struck up a conversation. The harpist had never seen this man before and wondered why a stranger should be so pleased to have met him. They talked of this and that, and then the stranger asked him what the most terrifying experience of his life had been?

Here was a subject the harpist enjoyed relating! He declared it was the petrifying encounter with a pack of wolves on the moor between Atholl and Strathardle.

The stranger urged him to tell him more and he described the freezing winter snow and being scared out of his wits to find himself alone and at the mercy of these wild animals. He explained he was a musician and having only his clarsach to hand to protect himself he decided to play the instrument in an effort to scare the animals away.

Alas, he told the stranger, this plan had not worked, but the wolves did not pounce or attack him. They formed the most extraordinary audience he had ever played before and then the leader, a massive beast with shining eyes, lifted its paw and he saw it was injured by a blackthorn.

'I pulled the barb from the beast's foot and it left me in peace. I could not believe it! It turned away and took the rest of the pack with it! To this day, I have never been so frightened for my life nor so grateful to be left alone in the snow, healthy, whole and safe!'

The gentleman stretched out his hand and turned it palm upwards, asking, 'Do you recognise this hand? It is the hand from which you plucked a thorn on that day.'

In utter bewilderment the harpist stared at the scar on the man's hand.

'How can this be?' he stammered, his eyes moving rapidly from the scar to the gentleman and back again many times.

'My stepmother hated me. She was a witch and she thrust that thorn in my hand and turned me into a wolf.' The gentleman's pale blue eyes shimmered with gratitude. 'I would still be in a wolf's form now if not for your bravery and kindness. Sir, I am truly glad we met today. Thank you.'

CREEPY GHOST STORY

This is the story of a haunting which happened near Blairgowrie in the days when a home with electricity and inside plumbing were just a hope for the future.

Late one evening, Lizzie Stewart finished her washing and hung it up on the kitchen pulley. She picked up the tin bath full of dirty water and carried it through to the corridor, laying it down to unlatch the door. Every night she threw it outside but this time she paused, filled with a skin-crawling feeling of dread.

It was the last day of March and she knew it would be dark but it was something else which caused her to stop; a creepy feeling. She decided to leave the bath in the lobby and as it was no bigger than a large oval bucket, she pushed it against the wall and stepped around it.

After shutting down the Tillie lamp in the kitchen, she went through to the main living room where a good fire was burning, sending bright orange light flickering round the walls. Andrew, her husband, was already in bed, still awake, lying with his hands clasped behind his head, gazing towards the mantelpiece. The children were sound asleep, tucked in at the other end of the big wall bed. As she did every night, Lizzie turned the paraffin lamp down low; she liked to keep a light in the room for the little ones and knew the firelight would soon die away.

It was exactly half past eleven when Lizzie climbed over her husband and slid under the covers on the wall side of the bed. She was very tired and closed her eyes straight away.

Some five or ten minutes later, she raised herself on an elbow and looked past her husband towards the other side of the room. An old woman was standing by the door. She was neat and very well dressed with her hair drawn back into a bun allowing no strands to escape, just straight back. The figure was clear enough but seemed smoky, blurry at the edges.

Lizzie couldn't scream, no sound would come at first but with a cry of 'Uh … uh … uh Andrew!' she fell back against her pillow and pulled the covers tight over her head.

Andrew didn't move a muscle. He said later he felt like a rabbit frozen in fear in the sight of a weasel. It was bright from the fire and very quiet in the room, just the tick-tock, tick-tock of the clock on the mantelpiece. He strained to hear any other sound. Nothing.

From the corner of his eye he knew something was moving across the room, getting closer. He kept his hands behind his head and his raised elbow was blocking most of his view to the side but he saw a shadow move, sailing over to stand at the bedside. Then the figure moved to peer down at the children. Turning its head, it slid up the side of the bed, leaning over Andrew to stare at where Lizzie was hiding under the covers.

Andrew kept his eyes fixed, but unfocused, on the mantelpiece and the clock. Then it looked straight at Andrew.

He looked directly back.

He could see the grey hair scraped back in a bun, was aware of the long skirt and smart clothes from the olden days but he could see no face. There was nothing where a face should be.

Her head dipped forward and Andrew thought he made out two dark eyes but his fear was so fierce that a terrible weakness came over him, as if his muscles were turning to jelly. The old woman raised her arms and reached towards him, hands outstretched towards his neck to choke him.

As he said later, he found himself thinking he must pull himself together, for he was in a jam here! Mustering his strength, he pulled his hands from behind his head and swiped out at the old woman.

She was suddenly just a shadow but such a dense black shadow that as she moved backwards, away from him, she blocked out the light from the fire. Then the cloudy mass began quivering and breaking up like a vapour, disappearing from the floor up until it shot up to the ceiling and changed into the form of a wee skeleton, a baby's skeleton.

Andrew lay motionless, staring at the bizarre apparition. He said it seemed to bob and dangle around from the ceiling like some sort of macabre child's toy on a piece of string. Then it vanished.

He jumped out of bed and ran through to the kitchen to fetch another lamp and more paraffin. As he stumbled about in the dark he stepped into the cold bathtub of water with his left foot; on hurrying back, he did the same with his right foot but was grateful to this for jolting him free from the grip of terror.

He lit the lamp and made a thorough check of the house, going to the door and calling to the dog to come. The dog was a big beast, a fighter if given the chance, but it stuck its tail between its legs and wouldn't stay in the house.

Not finding anything amiss in the rest of the house but still feeling the hairs rise on the back of his neck, Andrew crept back into bed and tucked the covers securely around himself and his family.

He lifted the blanket away from his wife's head, telling her they might be having to leave their home.

'Oh no, Andrew!' she whispered. 'Did ye see it too?'

'Aye,' he said, regretting his words for now he'd made her even more frightened. She dived back under the blankets.

'Lizzie,' he said, 'de ye feel the cold?'

'Aye,' she cuddled in close.

An icy draught was chilling the room despite the fire and shuttered windows. Andrew watched as the curtains lifted and swayed. He remembered, when he let the dog out again, seeing the still, silent evening and clear moonlit night outside. The wind was not a draught. The wind was inside the room, blowing around, whirling against the bed drapes, the table-cloth, and pulling puffs of smoke from the fire.

Then it stopped. The ghost was gone.

Andrew and his family left their home shortly afterwards and, to his knowledge, the house was later sold seven more times in as many years.

Mungo the Cobbler

Since Iron Age times and the years of the Picts, to when earliest memories were passed from generation to generation, Strathardle has been inhabited. This long, wide glen sweeps around a bulky mass of mountains from Logierait to the Bridge of Cally.

In the days when one of the King Georges sat on the throne of Great Britain, this glen was especially busy with travellers. Every week, on a Friday, a market took place in Kirkmichael and people gathered there from as far afield at Blair Atholl. They tramped along the winding track with their wares or livestock in rain or sun, all eager to exchange what they had for a living.

In summer the path was baked hard by the sun, a perfect basking place for deadly adders. In the winter it was often impassable with snow, when even the red deer hunkered down in the lee of rocks until starvation forced them to paw the frozen ground in search of a bite of heather. Few ventured there in blizzards and those who lived in dwellings in the Strath would shutter their doors and windows and cluster by their fires.

Early one dark Friday morning in autumn, Mungo Connacher, a cobbler, left his home in Tynreich to go to Kirkmichael. Ahead of him lay the long, strenuous walk of five hours or more, so, with his heavy basket strapped on his back, he set a steady pace. Dawn had not yet broken when he strode through the blackened streets of Pitlochry but he knew that if he was to secure a good pitch at the market he needed to be up on the high moors before the sun rose. With his head down and a frown furrowing his brow, he cut a serious, worried figure bent beneath his wares.

When he neared Kirkmichael he became just one of many hurrying folk converging on the hamlet, all eyes watching for the first sight of the old church tower. Cockerels were crowing, sheep baaing, cows lowing, all being driven or carried to the market.

Mungo was pleased to see his usual spot was free and after a refreshing drink of ale, he spread out a wide blanket and laid out his footwear, satchels and belts to tempt passers-by.

Trade appeared to go well and Mungo's basket was considerably lighter when he repacked it for his walk home that evening. Yet his long face and drooping shoulders told a different story. Although he had plenty of customers, they were not paying him all they should. Times were hard and everyone had an understandable excuse as to why they could not give him all the money at the time of purchase. This had been going on for a while and it was causing Mungo sleepless nights because his own needs were not being met.

The next morning, pale and tired, Mungo went to his neighbour and confided how worried he was about the lack of payments.

His neighbour, Rob na Feithe (Rob of the Muscles), listened to his friend's plight and offered advice. He, Rob, would accompany Mungo on a visit to the homes of all the customers who owed him money.

'Tell them I am your lawyer,' he said, 'tell them, you have handed your business affairs and collection of debts over to me.'

Mungo agreed and a few days later they set off together up to Strathardle. They made an unlikely couple; wee, wiry Mungo in his patched tweed jacket and leather breeches; big, brawny Rob na Feithe squeezed into a borrowed black wool coat, with a starched white cravat swathed around his throat.

At the first house, Mungo introduced his 'lawyer' and explained the debt they owed was now being handled by this gentleman. They left without receiving any money but were offered a slice of bread with the crofter's newly churned butter. Rob declined, but Mungo accepted the bread and put it in his pocket to eat later. At the second house they told the same story and the crofter's wife wrung her hands, pleading for more time to pay and inviting them to take a refreshment before leaving. Again, Rob declined and they left.

At a weaver's house, they were met with apologies and on being invited inside it was clear to see from the bare room and meagre stores on the shelves that the housewife's pleas of poverty were genuine.

The same thing happened at all the places they called. No money was forthcoming.

'What am I to do?' Mungo moaned when they made their way back towards Tynreich. 'These people are as poor as I am. I need to eat too, it is only fair that if they wear my shoes on their feet that I should be paid for them.' He stamped his feet, 'See my boots? Falling apart!'

Rob stopped and leaned against a sturdy boulder. 'Mungo, will you give me a bit of bread? I'm getting hungry.'

Mungo reached into his pocket and took out the slices of bread he'd been given at the first house and they shared it beside the stone, now called Mungo's Stone (Clach Mhungo).

Ten days later, Mungo found himself answering knocks on the door of his workshop over and over again.

The person who had no money had butter, the person with no butter had cheese, another with chickens had eggs, and another, who did not farm, had linen. His customers may not have had money but within two weeks of calling at their doors, Mungo had been fully repaid.

The Green Lady of Newton Castle

Back in the closing years of the seventeenth century a handsome young man by the name of Lord Ronald lived in Newton Castle in Blairgowrie. As he grew to adulthood he became the object of desire for many local girls but one, above all, became besotted with him.

Jane Drummond was considered by all to be a beauty. On seeing her own reflection in the looking glass she knew this to be true, but, try as she might, Lord Ronald never gave her a second glance.

If they met on the street Jane's heart would race and her cheeks flush pink with anticipation. He was always courteous and would pass a few words with her father, bow over her mother's hand and smile a polite acknowledgement to poor Jane. Nothing more. No spark of curiosity or admiration came to his clear blue eyes, while Jane could only struggle to compose herself against showing her keen disappointment.

When an invitation arrived for the family to attend a ball or celebration in young Lord Ronald's pretty little castle,

Jane would be thrown into a frenzy of excitement and preparation. All to no avail.

Desperate to impress the young man, she eventually resorted to seeking help from a local witch. How could she make Lord Ronald notice her and fall in love with her?

The witch gave her advice and without a moment's hesitation, Jane hurried off to carry out the prescribed set of instructions.

First, she was to gather grasses and bind them together to form a string. Then she must go to the hanging tree on Gallows Knowe and cut some branches from it, bind them together with the grasses and go down to the river.

Late that evening, Jane picked up her wand of grass and rowan boughs and made her way through Blairgowrie's shadowy streets and down to the banks of the River Ericht. Following the witch's words, she sought out the Corbies Stane, a large rock near Boat Brae, where she sat down. For a few moments she fought a rising fear, staring into the mass of water sliding down the riverbed. Bats were reeling overhead and diving to skim flies from the river's moving surface, black as treacle under the night sky. Then, she shut her eyes and settled down to endure the whole time of darkness without moving from the stone or even opening her eyes for the smallest peek.

Such was her yearning for Lord Ronald that despite the cold night air and strange noises of otters splashing in the shallows, or the eerie cries of hunting foxes and owls, Jane sat perfectly still. She felt a wind blowing, so fiercely that her clothes were being pushed and pulled around her and sometimes she heard high-pitched laughter, like tinkling breaking glass, mingling with the rippling river.

At daybreak, she opened her eyes to find she was transformed! The faeries had clad her in the finest green gown and she was filled with a feeling of beauty and enchantment. Immediately she ran to the castle and came upon Lord Ronald in the front courtyard, preparing to mount his horse.

He glanced towards her and then stopped dead in his tracks, his eyes opening in wonder. Within seconds he was at her side and before the day was over, they were betrothed.

Over the next few weeks, Jane was swept along on a wave of euphoria! Her dream was coming true; she was to be the wife of her heart's desire! Surrounded by her family and friends the wedding festivities were the happiest she could imagine until, in the middle of her first dance, she heard a voice in her ear.

She looked sharply over her shoulder. There was no one there.

Lord Ronald saw her look of dismay and became alarmed by the terror in her eyes and her sudden deathly white pallor. The voice was of the witch, telling Jane she could not wear the Witchin' Claith of Green without dire consequences. With a cry, Jane fainted into her husband's arms and died before help could be summoned.

The church could not allow Jane to be buried in the church-yard because she died while under the enchantment of a witch. Lord Ronald was heartbroken and laid his bride to rest behind the castle at Knockie Hill, but she did not stay there peacefully.

It is said locally that every Hallowe'en, Lady Jane's head-stone turns three times and her ghost rises from the grave. Her shimmering green phantom floats to Newton Castle where she searches for her true love, and some have heard her sweet voice singing sad, melodious ballads.

THE FINGER LOCK

There were once three brothers who stayed together in the family cottage.

The two older boys were grand at playing the pipes but the youngest one, Johnnie, couldn't play at all. Thinking themselves better than their wee brother the big boys bullied him badly and used him to slave away in the cottage and labour on the land.

The evening before the local Games, the older boys pulled out their belts and buckles to shine them up, and brushed out their plaid to make themselves as handsome as peacocks.

'We must git oor pipes tuned up and oor medals oot to pin oan oor jaikits,' the eldest laughed.

'Aye, Geordie,' the middle son grinned. 'We'll be addin' tae them the morrow.'

Johnnie was elbow deep in the washing bowl, scrubbing the pots from dinner. 'Can Ah come wi' ye an' see the pipers in their finery? Ah've nivver seen a Games and it must be a grand sicht.'

'Naw, whit wid we be daen wi' ye there?' Geordie sneered. 'Ye look a mess, an' a' the folks wid stare an' laugh!'

'Please, can Ah come,' Johnnie pleaded.

Geordie went over and hit him across the face. 'Ye ha'e the coo tae milk and tak tae the meadow, the byre tae muck oot, an' sticks tae break! We'll be in need o' a guid meal when we git hame sae ye'll stiy here an' get oan wi' it!'

Well, the next morning poor Johnnie watched with sad eyes as his brothers put their pipe boxes and paraphernalia into the trap, hitched up the pony and set off down the hill to Blairgowrie.

Johnnie milked the cow and led her to the lush meadow by the burn, throwing himself down in the grass to think of what he was missing.

Then he heard a wee voice asking, 'Whit's wrang wi' ye, Johnnie? Ye look awfy doon heartit.'

Johnnie propped himself up on his elbow and looked around. A faerie, like a wee green man, was sitting crosslegged just a few feet away.

The faerie was looking at him intently, head cocked to one side. 'Whit's wi' the lang face oan this sunny summer day?'

Johnnie explained about asking his brothers if he could join them at the Games and how they wouldn't let him.

'Ah'v nivver seen the Games,' he said pitifully, 'an' Ah'd fair love tae see the spectacle o' the pipers an' the caber tossing an' the hammer throwin' … they jist keep me tae dae a' the chores an' … they hit me.'

'Nivver mind,' the faerie soothed, 'I'll play ye a tune.'

'But they've taken the pipes …'

The little green man reached above his head and plucked a thick blade of grass. 'I din nae need pipes! This straw will dae fine fur a faerie tae play a tune.'

With that, he placed it between his lips and sent up the sweetest, clearest Strathspey Johnnie had ever heard. The notes danced on into a lively reel, accompanied by the rippling waters of the burn and the gentle rustle of the aspens.

'Noo then,' the faerie said, 'I shouldn't be holdin' ye back frae the Games. Gae up tae the hoose and git yersel' dressed an' pick up yer pipes. Yer gaun tae play better than ye've heard frae me!'

'Och naw,' Johnnie was appalled. 'Ah cannae even play the chanter!'

'Ye'll play jist grand! Hurry noo, up tae the hoose an' git ready.'

'But whit aboot the coo?'

'I'll watch o'er the coo.'

Johnnie raced to the cottage door then stopped, 'Aw naw! They lock the door when they gae oot fur they think Ah'll eat all the meat …'

The faerie was beside him saying calmly, 'Blow yer breath on the lock, Johnnie, an' pit yer' wee finger in the lock an' gie it a turn and the door will open.'

Johnnie leaned in close to the door handle and blew on the lock, twisting his pinkie in where the key should turn and the locked clicked open!

'Noo, gae tae the back room and pull oot the big kist frae 'neath the bed.'

Johnnie had never known about this old chest and heaved it out from under the bedstead. It was covered in cobwebs and dust but when he lifted the lid he could hardly believe his eyes. There were kilts and straps, buckles and pipes, but not like any pipes he'd seen before. These were solid gold.

The faerie helped him dress and everything fitted perfectly. On catching sight of himself in the window glass, oh, he looked handsome and proud!

'Now tune yer pipes afore ye go,' the faerie cried.

Then Johnnie's face fell, 'This is all well an' guid, an' Ah'm gratefu' tae ye fur cheering me up, but Ah can nae play, so Ah can nae gae tae the Games.'

'Ye can play,' the faerie said firmly, hopping up on the dresser to speak eye to eye. 'Ah'm tellin' ye, ye can play.'

'Ah hear ye,' Johnnie nodded and placed the pipes on his shoulder and tuned up.

The sound was glorious! He played and played and could not stop.

'That'll dae!' shouted the faerie, and Johnnie obeyed with smiling eyes and a heaving chest.

The faerie gave him a serious look, 'There's one pibroch I want ye tae play, an' that's the Finger Lock. Ye recall ye blew yer breath on the lock and pit yer wee finger in the lock? Well, there's yer tune. An' that's the name ye'll cry it, The Finger Lock.'

Johnnie nodded but seeing a shadow of disbelief in his eyes, the faerie repeated his instruction, giving heavy meaning to each word.

'That's the name ye'll call it, this new pibroch. Ye'll play it. Jist work yer fingers when ye gae oan stage an' ye'll play the Finger Lock. If they ask ye whit the name is of this new pibroch, you've got to tell them the Finger Lock.'

Johnnie agreed and rushed to hitch the trap to the old mare in the byre and hasten down to the Games. He was the last piper on the stage and when he put the pipes on his shoulder he remembered all the faerie told him.

The audience fell silent, lost in the magical music of this newcomer's strathspeys, reels and his new pibroch. His performance completed, the applause and cheers rang out and the judges stepped forward to shake Johnnie's hand.

'My guidness, ye can play man! What pibroch is that, the last yin?'

'That's the Finger Lock, sir,' replied Johnnie.

'It's a new one?'

'Aye, sir, 'tis ma own composition.'

The faerie had warned Johnnie to leave the Games before his brothers so he could be safely home and have the pipes away before they returned.

It was late when the older brothers came rattling up the track. They saw Johnnie in the byre, as usual, dressed in his tattered smock and leggings, and left him to unhitch the trap and settle the pony for the night.

When he went inside he found them sitting about, muttering to one another about not bothering to go to the Games ever again.

'How were the Games?' he asked, struggling to keep the smile from his voice.

'There wis a guid piper, the like we've nivver seen afore. Ah'll not be pipin' there agin, nor others Ah've heard say. Man, he was some piper!'

'An' whit did he play?' Johnnie asked.

'Och he played the strathspeys we ken, but he played them *better*, ye ken … an' he played a pibroch the like of which no one's heard. The Finger Lock, he cried it.'

'The Finger Lock?' Johnnie beamed. 'Guid God, man, Ah can play that masel'!'

'Dinnae be daft, ye can nae!' Geordie shouted.

'Gie me yer pipes an' Ah'll play it!' Johnnie reached for his brother's pipe box.

'Ye will no! Leave ma pipes alane!'

'Ah'll play oan ma ane pipes then,' said Johnnie and went to the kist in the back room.

The next thing the two brothers heard was the tuning up of pipes and then Johnnie coming through the house to march up and down in front of them playing the Finger Lock. They sat in stunned silence, mouths wide open, eyes agog.

From that day on, the elder brothers did not go to the Games. It was Johnnie who played the pipes at the Games, travelling far and wide and taking all the prizes wherever he took to the stage. He spent his life delighting folk throughout the country with tunes from his golden pipes, especially the crowd's favourite, the Finger Lock.

A Stony Dilemma

Mhairi, the youngest child and only daughter of a Perthshire Laird, was faced with a terrible dilemma. A local landowner, Archibald Orr, wished to marry her and she was appalled by the very thought of such a union.

It was not the fact he was old, although there were more than two decades between them, nor that he was fat, she knew several plump gentlemen who were pleasant company. No, when he courted her it was the shifty glint in his eye and the barely disguised, unsavoury innuendoes which made her shudder.

One day, her father told her Mr Orr had called on him to ask for her hand in marriage. Mhairi held her breath, hoping the request was not granted. However, as her father explained, this was not a suitor to easily reject because Mr Orr was a very wealthy, influential man with fingers in many pies.

'I wish it was different, my dear daughter,' her father said, solemnly, 'but you could do worse? He owns substantial property in Edinburgh and is entertained in all the great houses in our land. As his wife, you would want for nothing money could buy, which would give me comfort as I grow older.'

Mhairi sought out her mother who was usually sympathetic to her point of view, and declared she would refuse Mr Orr's offer of matrimony. To her surprise, her mother patted the seat beside her and they spoke at length. She genuinely wished Mhairi to be happy but for the sake of the estate and her older brothers, whose fortunes depended on good relations with this powerful businessman, her mother agreed with her father that the marriage would be advantageous.

Mhairi had a duty to her family not to offend Mr Orr, a point which was made particularly clear.

So Mhairi watched with dread when Orr's carriage arrived at their front door. She thought of pleading illness and staying in her room but, as a devoted daughter, she appeared in the drawing room when summoned and accepted the gentleman's low bow with a polite nod.

'My dear,' her mother greeted her, smiling a little too brightly. 'We have the honour of Mr Orr's presence and, given the sunshine today, he would like you to join him for a walk in the garden. I shall wait on the terrace and have refreshments brought out for us all to enjoy.'

No sooner were they alone in the formal flower garden than her portly beau stepped in front of her to block her way.

'I am sure your father has appraised you of my intentions. Please relieve me of my suspense and give me your answer? Will you be my wife?'

'My goodness!' Mhairi cried. 'Such a momentous question from a man as important and rich as yourself!'

He feigned humility at the compliment, a smug expression bunching his chubby cheeks.

'It is quite overwhelming, sir,' she continued with a nervous laugh. 'I beg your patience for I am yet young and feel inadequate to respond.'

A frown clouded his features. How dare she not accept at once! To cover his rising temper he stepped aside and they resumed their walk along the path.

'Well now,' he said suddenly, 'let us leave the matter to Fate, eh? What do you say?'

Taking a small drawstring bag from his pocket, he emptied it of coins and dangled it in front of her. 'This path has brown stones and white stones, has it not?'

Mhairi nodded, her heart sinking: what was his game?

'I shall place one brown and one white stone in the bag. If you pick out a brown stone, you marry me. If it is a white stone, I shall not ask again.'

He leaned down to collect the stones although his sizeable paunch and arthritic knees made it a slow, awkward manoeuvre. To her horror, Mhairi saw him scoop up two brown stones and slip them quickly into the bag.

'Now, no peeking,' he teased, proffering the bag, 'avert your eyes and take your pick!'

She obeyed, but on pulling her hand from the bag she fumbled and the stone fell to the ground.

'Oh my!' she cried, 'how clumsy of me! Forgive me, sir. Now it is lost among all the other brown and white stones …' she looked up at him with candid eyes. 'Never mind, the answer is easy to find for whichever stone is still in your bag, I must have chosen the other.'

THE WEE BIRD

Many years ago in a market town in Perthshire, a mother called her daughter in from playing and told her to take a jug up to the dairy and have it filled with milk.

'Can I take my skipping rope with me?' the little girl asked.

The mother was a bad-tempered woman and snapped back, 'No, you can't!'

'Oh please, please, I will be very careful and won't spill a drop of milk.'

The mother grudgingly agreed, shouting after her, 'If you spill the milk or break my jug, I'll kill ye!'

The little girl skipped all the way to the dairy at the top of the town and got the jug filled with fresh, foamy milk. On the way back she struggled to hold the wooden handles of her rope and balance the jug so not to drip a drop. Suddenly, the jug slipped from her hands and fell to the ground, breaking into many pieces.

The girl set about finding another jug and a kindly old lady, seeing the child's despair, took a close look at the fragments on the path.

'I have the very neighbour of this jug. Dinnae fret, dearie, you can have mine.'

The little girl thanked her politely and hurried off to get more milk. She was very cautious over every step on the way home, keeping her skipping rope wrapped up tightly and held securely in her hand.

Her mother took the jug from her daughter and was about to place it in the larder when she stopped.

'This is not my jug!' She turned to her daughter, raising her eyebrows accusingly. 'This is a different jug.'

'No it's not, that's the same one as ye gave me,' the girl said.

'This is not my jug. Mine had a red line round the top and this one has a blue line.'

So, her mother killed her.

She baked her in a pie for the family meal that night. When the father came home he asked where his daughter was and his wife told him she was out playing. Their two sons came home and the family sat round the table enjoying the warm smell of pastry and meaty gravy.

'Call the lass in from her playing,' the father said, 'we are all wanting to eat.'

'Let her play,' said the mother, cutting through the pastry lid and doling out the pie.

Then the father stopped chewing and pushed the meat around on his dish, revealing a little finger with a silver ring. He demanded to know what happened and his wife told him the story.

'Now look what you've done!' he cried. 'I've a guid mind tae kill *you* an' all!'

The sons were very upset as well but in the end the father decided not to kill the mother.

There was a heavy snowfall that year just before Christmas and a little bird appeared at the window, peeping in from the cold. The boys took pity on it and fed it crumbs when their mother wasn't looking (she was very strict and after what she did to their sister, they were fearful of her temper).

On Christmas night a voice came down the chimney, 'Brother, brother! Look up, look up and see what I have brought you!'

The youngest boy stuck his head into the hearth and down came toys and sweets. The voice called again for the other brother and he too was showered with toys and sweets.

'Father, father! look up and see what I've got!'

The father knelt at the grate and looked up. He received a new jacket and a sealed letter with the words 'Don't open this letter until two hours after Christmas night.'

'Mother, mother,' the voice echoed down the chimney again, 'look up and see what I have!'

The mother thrust her head into the open hearth and a large stone dropped on her skull, killing her instantly.

The father wrapped his wife up in a blanket and they cleared up the mess as best they could until two hours had passed and they could open the letter.

'Dear Father,' it said, 'this is your little daughter. The spell is broken once I have killed mother, I shall come back to you on New Year's Eve.'

So, on New Year's Eve the father and his sons waited in the house all day. They waited and waited and she did not come. Then, at three minutes to midnight, a knock came on the window and they ran to open it.

The wee brown bird hopped inside, saying, 'Father, brothers! I'm home again!'

'Why,' the father burst out, 'you're the little bird now!'

'I know, but if you take my mother's pinkie off her right hand, I shall change back to being a girl.'

The father hurried off to where he buried his wife and cut off the little finger on her right hand which still held a silver pinkie ring. He ran home and, on seeing his daughter was no longer a bird but the little brown-haired child he loved, the whole family cheered.

The girl took her mother's ring and placed it in a box beside the silver ring she used to wear herself, telling them, 'Mother wasn't really bad, it was the Devil that was inside her, and now she's dead she will be in Heaven.'

And the family lived happily ever after.

The Challenge

The farmer walked round his farm and land, he loved it all and had been there all his life. However, a question vexed him, what would happen when he was gone? Tradition dictated that it should be evenly divided between his three children, but he couldn't bear the thought of his treasured land being split up into small plots. Besides, on its own the farm made a good enough living, but divided into three it would be difficult to sustain anyone, let alone a family. But who to give it to? His eldest son, a born craftsman but no real affinity for the land; his middle child, a practical, sensible and clever boy; or his youngest, a girl always full of joy and love for everyone and everything.

He pondered and pondered until he came up with an unusual solution. He called his children together and explained.

'I'll give you a year, at the end of the year you must come with your answer. The most successful will be the farm owner after me.'

His sons and daughter looked at each other in puzzlement, what was their father planning?

He went on: 'The big, old barn out the back.'

'The biggest?' said the eldest

'Yes,' he continued. 'Well, I want you to fill it so it stays filled.'

'What with?' queried the younger brother.

'Ah,' said the father, 'that is up to you.'

They had a year to work out how to fill the old barn permanently? That would be easy they thought, they would keep it stocked with hay.

'Constantly full,' said the father. And that was the challenge.

Immediately, the eldest asked leave to go to the city where he would be bound to find an answer. His father consented and the younger son and daughter stayed, the boy with furrowed brow and the girl looking thoughtful.

Months went by and the brother and sister stayed on the farm helping their father, until one day the brother went to his father to ask leave to travel. He had been thinking and was sure he had an answer but needed to learn how to make it work. His father consented and off he went.

So the father and daughter remained on the farm. She seemed happy to be there and was always off to see someone in her free time, or run an errand for one of the old folk or someone would drop by for a blether. She seemed perfectly happy with her life, but in no way trying to find an answer.

Her father waited until he could stand it no more; the year was almost over when he called his daughter to him.

'Daughter, do you not accept the challenge? Do you not want to stay on the farm?'

'Oh Faither, more than anything.'

'But why do you not seek an answer like your brithers?'

'Everything I need is already here,' she replied.

Time passed quickly enough and soon the year was up.

A great line of carts was seen approaching the farm. The farmer came out in amazement and there at the head was his eldest son.

'Faither, I've been apprenticed to a mattress maker and have found an answer.' He waved his hand at the carts. 'My master asked me to stay but when I couldn't, he gave me these as a gift.'

And with that he leapt down from the cart and grabbed a large sack off the back. He called to the other cart drivers to do the same and soon they were all in the barn surrounded by sacks.

'Watch as I fill the barn, Faither!' He opened one of the sacks and the others followed suit and at his signal they all shook their bags. Soon the barn was full of feathers. Feathers everywhere, big ones, small ones, but all white. It was like a soft, fluffy snowfall. The barn was filled with them reaching right up to the ceiling and so it stayed for a while. But then they began to slowly drift down until they became a big pile on the floor: the barn was full no more.

Before anything could be said, there was a loud whistle and there was the younger brother striding along the path with a pack on his back. His father and brother smiled and welcomed him. He saw the goose feathers on the floor and with the help of all of them they cleared the feathers away. Night was beginning to draw in and the young man stepped forward. He took from his pack a long, thin, carefully wrapped package.

'I've been working with a candle maker,' he explained, 'experimenting with ways to make candles last longer, and this is my finest result.'

He took off the wrapping and there was a tall, white candle with a long wick. He put the candle in the middle of the barn and lit it. Soon there was a beautiful, pure light shining into every corner and space in the barn. It continued glowing long after normal candles would die. But after a while, a long while, the candle began to fade and splutter and the light grew dimmer until it finally went out and they were in darkness.

The father was thinking deeply: each son had come up with a good solution but who should win? Just as he was puzzling over this there was a burst of chatter and laughter and his daughter appeared, surrounded by her many friends. They were carrying sticks of wood, water, a kettle and mugs.

'I'm here to try my luck, Faither,' she said.

He was surprised; he thought she'd given up. The daughter and her friends quickly built a fire, blethering the whole time. Tea was made and drunk and the barn filled with the sound of laughter and fun. People came and went, more tea was made, bannocks eaten and still the barn was full of voices laughing, joking and talking. This carried on for many hours and showed no sign of abating when the farmer stepped forward.

'Enough, you all should get back to yer ain hames,' and off they went.

He turned to look at his three children and suddenly gave a great big smile. The choice was simple.

To his eldest he said, 'The feathers were a good idea and your master must have valued you highly to give you so many. Return to him and continue your trade.'

The eldest son beamed, he wanted nothing more.

To his younger son, 'The candle was like nothing I have seen, you should continue this work and see if you can develop it further.'

To his daughter, 'You have reminded me of the most important things in the world: life and love. The farm is yours.'

The girl smiled and threw her arms around her father. From that day, the door was always open, a welcome to any traveller, many a ceilidh was held there and the farm was always full of life, love and laughter.

THE GIANTS OF GLEN SHEE

Glen Shee or Gleinn Sith, the glen of the Faeries, is hauntingly beautiful when the weather is being kind to mortals. As a place to live and tend livestock it can be cruel and formidable. Legends and tales of faeries, witches and giants abound in this desolate landscape where massive mountains tower on either side of moorland and the River Shee flows down to the Blackwater.

A long time ago, the locals were frequently terrorised by giants who lived in the glen.

Two giants in particular, Collie Cam and his wife, were a very bad-tempered pair, always causing trouble and making the crofters' lives a misery. It seemed they could not agree upon anything and their bickering would erupt into an awful noise; shouting and pelting one another with whatever came to hand. Boulders and stones littered the valley and after a night of enduring the crashes and yells of a spectacular fight, the local folk would emerge to inspect the damage left in the giants' wake. Many told of days of labour gathering animals from the glen because they escaped from knocked down sheep folds or smashed byres.

One night the couple became so enraged that Collie Cam seized an enormous stone and held it above his head, threatening to hurl it at his wife. She continued to goad him but just as he was about to launch it towards her, the stone broke in two.

One half flew through the air and landed in Blackwater and the other half came down in Glenisla at Clachnockatur. If you are passing Collie Cam's Stane in Blackwater or the Warrior's Stone in Glenisla, you may hear a growling and rumbling. Perhaps it is the water, but perhaps, as locals have said for centuries, it is Collie Cam and his wife still at it hammer and tongs!

Another tale about a pair of giants comes from further north in Glen Shee. These two were great lumbering men, each believing they were stronger than the other.

A young lad, who often struggled to sleep through the din made by the giants, lay on his heather and thistledown mattress in a croft, listening to the commotion beyond the walls. His mother worked hard to make the family comfortable and keep tasty food in the larder and his father worked tirelessly tending the animals, cutting peat and curing furs to make a living. Yet their simple, content lives were blighted by the giants.

Enough was enough! The lad jumped up from his bed and went outside.

'Why are you always fighting?' he shouted up to the giants. 'If you want to find out which of you is stronger, why not have a throwing competition?'

The giants agreed and the boy pointed out two small rocks, and told them both to throw them and see who threw the furthest. The rocks were like pebbles to the giants and they threw them so far away down the glen it was impossible to see who had won. The boy pointed out two larger rocks and again the giants tried to outdo one another and again it was hard to see the winner. By now the giants were getting very competitive and picking up bigger and bigger rocks and hurling them across the moor.

'You are both very strong,' the boy urged. 'Who will be the winner?'

One of the giants seized a great boulder and balanced it on his head, 'I am!' he cried, and thumped it down on the other giant's head, killing him.

The glen was peaceful for a long time after that.

As you make your way through the glen, look out for the scattered rocks from this deadly competition, you can still see them lying among the heather.

WESTWARD BOUND

THE WEE SPECKLED STONE

Near the little village of Dull there stands the fine stone house of Fincastle, where the Stewart family lived since the early years of the seventeenth century. At the time of this story it was inhabited by a Colonel Stewart and his family. Befitting his status in the local community the colonel's wife and servants could be counted on to keep it clean and wholesome should unexpected visitors call.

Then something strange began to happen.

A tapping and bumping was heard, like someone rapping their knuckles on the floor, knocking each step of the wooden staircase and clattering on the pans and pots in the kitchen.

A day or so after this was first noticed a maid discovered the source of the commotion. While sweeping beneath a chair, her broom caught a stone and sent it skittering across the flagstone floor. The sound was exactly the same as she knew so well from being woken in the night.

It was a brown, grey and white speckled stone, bigger than a pebble but smaller than a rock. It was too big to have become lodged in the pads of a dog's paw or the sole of a boot, or even caught in the hem of her mistress's skirts.

Wondering how it came to be in the house, the maid reached down to pick it up. She let out a great shriek, flinging down her broom and rushing behind the high-backed settle. The stone had jumped clean out of her hand and bounced away. Her cries brought Mrs Stewart to her side and through shuddering sobs the maid told her what happened.

'It's just a stone,' her mistress chided, chuckling. 'Throw it outside and get on with your work.'

'Ah'll no' touch yon stane again!' the girl cried.

So Mrs Stewart picked it up, walked through to the back scullery and threw it out the door.

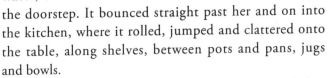

The household slept soundly that night, undisturbed by any annoying bangs and knocks. The following day, when the maid unlatched the back door to fetch the morning water, the stone was on the doorstep. It bounced straight past her and on into the kitchen, where it rolled, jumped and clattered onto the table, along shelves, between pots and pans, jugs and bowls.

This time the maid was so concerned her mistress's fine china or glass vases might be broken that she quite forgot to be frightened. A chase ensued, but the wee speckled stone was always just out of reach.

'Mercy, what a to do!' Mrs Stewart scolded, coming on the lively scene to find her maid balanced on the table, reaching up high towards the platter rack on the wall.

At that moment the stone dropped from the rack, bounced its zig-zagging way over the floor and off towards the front hallway. Both maid and mistress stared in amazement, mouths gaping, until Mrs Stewart remembered her manners and politely pressed the back of her hand to her lips.

They moved from room to room, mesmerised by the spritely little stone until their dismay turned to laughter.

'It is very entertaining!' Mrs Stewart told her husband. 'Indeed, it looks as if it is dancing ... and not one single cup or glass has been broken despite it springing around the kitchen like a demented bumble bee!'

Whether Colonel Stewart agreed with his wife, or even saw the stone for himself is not known; however, the racket it made that night caused Mrs Stewart to review its charms.

'The stone must be put out of the house,' she decided.

This was no easy task. With the speckled stone finally caught, cupped between two hands and taken outside, the maid was instructed to walk a good distance down the lane before throwing it into the hedgerow.

The next morning it was back on the doorstep.

Ever more inventive precautions were taken to block its way into the house but it always managed to enter. In the evenings the palaver was reversed with Mrs Stewart and her maid trying creative ways to get rid of the stone. It was buried, thrown into the river, pushed deep down a rabbit hole, dropped in the well, but it always appeared again the next morning.

Eventually, Mrs Stewart accepted her defeat in a compromise: every night it was thrown outside and every morning it returned. She regained her pleasure in watching its curious antics and, as for the wee speckled stone, it is said to have happily cavorted around Fincastle for many years.

THE GABHAR

A young gardener, who had been away working in the south, was due to return to Killichonan for a celebration with his relatives. The ceilidh came and went and there was no sign of him. As the days went on, the villagers became anxious for his wellbeing. They discovered that he stopped for refreshments at Coshieville and must have taken the road around Schiehallion from Rannoch to Aberfeldy, but there were no further sightings of him. Their fears were heightened when they received a message from the Seer of Rannoch. She told them to look around the loch above Crossmount, where her vision showed a pale, clothed shape in the rushes.

Sadly, when a search party scoured the banks of that place, they came upon the young man's remains. As soon as they pulled his body from the water it was clear he had not died from drowning. Even the most stoic men in the group turned away from the grisly sight, retching; others stared, aghast. The pale torso lying on the pebble shore was bloodless, washed by the water. It had been badly nibbled by fish but clearly showed he had been disembowelled, one arm and a leg below the knee were missing and the side of his face was ripped to shreds.

'It was the Gabhar!' one man murmured. 'Look at the scratches.'

'He must have tried to cross the river after dark … he should have been warned.'

No local person would attempt to enter that ford after the sun fell below the horizon, it was a lesson scolded and drummed into their children from taking their first steps. Brave men possessing excellent skills with sword and dirk had been killed by the Gabhar. It was a creature of terrifying stature and strength, being part goat, part wildcat, part man, capable of ripping its victim limb from limb and gouging out their innards.

'This is a terrible thing, terrible,' one of the dead man's relatives moaned, 'and now I have the awful task of telling my brother the fate of his eldest son.'

On hearing the news, a member of the family swore revenge for the killing and set off to find the Gabhar. He was a tall, athletically built man from Lochaber, Cailein Suil Duhb (Colin Black-Eyes). His long strides made short work of the miles, bringing him to the ford while the sun was still dipping in the sky. Goats called from the hillside, larks sang their melodious song, mingling with the breeze rustling through the heather. The scene was so peaceful he doubted if this was the spot of the savage attack and, looking around, struck off up a track to a cottage.

A knock on the door brought an old man, a weaver, to his aid. Oh aye, he was told, the Gabhar was a frightful beast and no one should attempt to cross the ford after sunset. The weaver grew very concerned when Colin told him he planned to do just that: cross the ford in darkness.

'You'll die! A fine young man like yersel', think o' yer mither, would she no' be broken hairted? Cross the noo,' he urged, 'or wait until sunrise.'

'No. It is my duty to avenge my cousin's death and I shall succeed.'

'It is said tae be larger than ony animal ye can imagine – a man's strength alone is no' enough. How will ye defend yerself agin yon creature?'

'I have my gun and it will be primed with dry powder.'

'An' if ye miss and have nae time tae reload?'

'I have my sword!'

'And if the sword breaks or jams in its scabbard?'

'Then I also have the bana-chait cul na cruachan (the cat behind the hip) to call upon,' Colin Black-Eyes laughed, winking at the old man's confused expression. 'Dinnae fret auld man, I shall not be dying this night!'

When dusk fell, Colin made his way to the ford. Holding his pistol at the ready, he stepped into the water rushing over smooth, slippery stones. Within seconds the creature reared up just yards ahead, water streaming down its towering goat-like body, yet the arms reaching towards him were those of a cat, sheathing and unsheathing its claws. Incredulous, his heart pounding, Colin used both hands to steadily take aim and pull the trigger. The gun did not fire.

The Gabhar came pouncing towards him.

Colin grabbed for his sword but it would not budge from the scabbard and the beast was now upon him, biting with pointed teeth, its feline claws grasping and slicing at his body. Colin reached for his 'cat behind the hip', his dirk, and stabbed at the beast, driving the blade into its side and then its chest. It screamed and fell to all fours, scuttling and splashing through the shallows to vanish into the black hillside.

Colin, bleeding, but thankful to be alive, limped back up the hill to the weaver's cottage to seek bandages. His desperate knocks at the door were ignored so he lifted the latch and entered, finding the old man lying on the bed groaning. By the light of the fire, Colin could see a dark stain spreading across the man's chest. He took out his dirk and approached the bedside.

Up jumped the old man! Blood seeped through the clothing on his chest and down his side, exactly where Colin wounded the Gabhar. For a moment they stared at each other and Colin knew the weaver was a witch who could cast a spell over any weapon rendering it useless, as long as he knew the nature of the weapon before it was used.

With the speed of a youth, the weaver fled through the door and up the hill. Colin raced after him.

On reaching the summit, the bent old man transformed into the terrifying horned creature, rising up on his hind legs and roaring. Colin charged towards it, ramming the dirk straight into its heart.

The Gabhar collapsed, crumpling into a heap with a raw, wailing scream. To make sure it was dead, Colin hacked off its head and hurried down to the loch, where he threw it far into the murky depths.

There have been no incidents with the Gabhar since that day, but the local name for that winding road over Schiehallion is the 'Goat Track'.

A BIT OF LAND

Campbell of Glenorchy dismounted from his horse and handed the reins to a stable boy at the inn.

'There'll be a thre'penny bit for ye,' he shouted through the heavy rain, 'if ye keep that saddle dry along with the horse!'

Water poured from the sky, drenching trees, streaming off the roofs into Killin's streets and pooling in bubbling puddles in every dip and rut. Under his wide-brimmed hat, Campbell bowed his head and splashed his way towards the courthouse. On reaching the shelter of the inner hallway, he looked down at his boots: soaked and mud splattered.

When the court adjourned for the day he made his way back to the inn to take some food before riding home. There, in a corner booth, he spied MacNab of Kinnell, the gentleman who owned most of the local land. Asking if he could join him, they fell into conversation and it was not long before Campbell brought up a subject he had mused over all day.

'With the court being in Killin, sir, it would be useful to me to have a place to tether my horse. Would you sell me a bit of land at Finlarig?'

MacNab was a canny businessman and interested in any chance to make a profit, so he enquired how much land Campbell was seeking.

'The length and breadth of a thong?'

'Are you sure? Is that sufficient? It seems a very small bit.'

Campbell narrowed his eyes. 'Yes,' he confirmed, 'that would suffice.'

MacNab made a few quick calculations and reckoned he could get away with asking a slightly inflated sum for such a small patch because of the value of convenience to the gentleman.

The price was agreed and they shook hands on the deal.

Campbell went off and found the largest hide in the county, which he took to a skilful cobbler and asked him to cut the entire hide into one long continuous strip, the width of a shoelace.

It was a mighty task, but the shoemaker rose to the challenge. With practised hands, he spread the great piece of leather on his workbench and set to work cutting from the very edge. It took many hours of painstaking work. People gathered around, lamps were lit when the sun set, meat and ale were brought by womenfolk to keep up his strength and everyone held their breath when he tackled difficult corners. How terrible would it be if his knife slipped? Eventually, after sharpening his blade repeatedly, he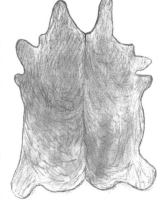

reduced the hide to a large coiled pile of yards and yards of narrow thong.

Piling the thong into a basket, Campbell rode to Finlarig to measure out his piece of land. In order to prove he was not taking more than agreed, he requested MacNab to be present.

MacNab watched in astonishment as the lengthy leather string was laid out, first lengthwise and then across the breadth of the land adjacent to the track. He could not argue with Campbell's measurements and Campbell claimed his land.

This was the first piece of MacNab land to be purchased by a Campbell, but it certainly wasn't the last. Little by little, the Campbells succeeded in taking all land owned by the MacNabs.

THE KISSING GHOST

In the heart of Scotland, north of mighty Ben Lawers, lies one of the longest and most beautiful valleys in Scotland: Glen Lyon. The River Lyon twists and turns through moorland and mountains for over thirty-five miles, pooling in Loch Lyon before surging on to join the Tay and flow out to the east coast.

With few human inhabitants in this vast wilderness, it might be supposed that any deed committed by man could be hidden. This would be a mistake.

In the middle of Glen Lyon stands Castle Meggernie. The original stark, five-storey tower built by Mad Colin Campbell 500 years ago was extended with the addition of a striking mansion house, gardens and a fine arboretum. It presents a faerie-tale appearance to those who pass by, belying the vicious deeds carried out within its walls.

Here, reality merges with the supernatural in one of Scotland's most thought-provoking hauntings.

Nearly 1,000 years ago the Macgregor clan claimed this remote glen, but in the reign of David I the Campbells took possession, driving the Macgregors north to Rannoch. It was in Meggernie Castle, then called Glenlyon, that the notorious Captain Robert Campbell hatched his murderous plan to massacre the MacDonalds in Glencoe. Then through marriages and alliances, in the 1700s Meggernie moved into the ownership of the Menzies of Culdares.

At the time of our story nearly 100 years had passed since it was held in Menzies' hands and, after various owners, the castle belonged to an Englishman, Herbert Woods.

Queen Victoria was on the throne and it was thought a grand adventure to tour the Scottish Highlands like Her Majesty, therefore an invitation from the Woods was one to be embraced! Ladies enjoyed strolls along avenues of gigantic lime trees planted by James Menzies, a renowned arborist in his time, or took tea in the formal flower gardens. Gentlemen indulged in deer stalking or a spot of fly fishing in the trout-laden river just yards from the door.

One such house party in 1862 included E.J. Simons and Beaumont Fetherstone, the latter of the two an avid diarist. The two men travelled separately to Castle Meggernie and were introduced to each other for the first time by the Woods. Arriving late in the evening, they were both relieved to have completed the long journey.

Large though the castle was, every one of the bedrooms in the main house was filled. To provide separate sleeping accommodation for Fetherstone and Simons their hostess instructed the maids to prepare the two bedrooms in the square tower; the oldest part of the castle. These rooms were rarely used but with fires in the grate, a good supply of candles and well aired blankets and mattresses, they were made ready.

Simons and Fetherstone were intrigued by their rooms. The castle's five-foot-thick walls, slit windows and heavy oak doors were a novelty to the southerners, but they were puzzled by a blocked-up doorway between their two rooms. On Fetherstone's side, there was an alcove set deep in the wall, while on Simons' side the wall was blocked off immediately behind the redundant door.

It was odd, but nothing more, and they bid each other good night in a jovial mood and retired to their respective bedchambers. Within moments of blowing out their candles, they fell into a deep sleep.

Suddenly, Simons was shocked awake by excruciating pain searing through his cheek.

Gasping and flailing his arms in agony, he sat bolt upright, not daring to touch the side of his face. It was consumed by a terrible burning, as if branded by a red-hot iron. He stared about him in confusion, heart pounding, eyes bulging at a movement in the shadows.

The shimmering image of the upper half of a young woman floated towards the wall and disappeared through the blocked doorway.

Frightened out of his wits, Simons fumbled for his matches, succeeding at last to calm his hands enough to light a candle. He held it high. The room was empty. Opening his dressing case he braced himself for what he would see in the mirror. Surely this intense pain would mean permanent disfigurement? The burn felt deep, scorching through the flesh to the very bone itself.

There was no mark, his skin was smooth above the line of his beard.

There was no more sleep for Simons that night. In the morning, he waited impatiently in the corridor outside their rooms and the moment Fetherstone appeared, he started to tell him of his nightmarish ordeal. Fetherstone stopped him mid-flow, beseeching him to say no more because he too had a remarkable tale to tell. This agreed, they sought out their host and related their stories independently.

As Fetherstone recorded in his diary, he woke to a purple light flooding the room. He could see a female figure standing at the foot of his bed and, befuddled with sleep, thought she must be a maid or house guest walking in her sleep. The woman slid smoothly round the side of the bed and leaned towards him, as if to kiss him. Startled, Fetherstone pulled sharply away, causing her to withdraw. Then, watching her drift towards the blocked doorway, the hairs rose up on the back of his neck: she was invisible below her waist. A second later, the phantom vanished.

The Woods were very interested in the astonishingly similar accounts of such an extraordinary event. They did not disbelieve the stories for one moment, although they admitted neither of them had personally seen anything untoward in the castle. However, this sighting by Simons and Fetherstone corroborated a series of incidents over the years which Mrs Woods found very trying.

It was difficult to keep staff, she confided, adding a plea to her guests not to speak of this most recent occurrence when the maids were present. They were nervous enough, she said, having already come to her with tales of seeing a strange, ghostly figure in the corridor leading out of the square tower. One maid resigned her job and ran from the castle after describing seeing the lower portion of a woman, her skirts swishing over the flagstones at each slow, measured step, but there was no torso or head. The creature's body appeared sliced in two with a blood-encrusted, jelly-like mass where her waist should be.

As several of the guests were leaving that day, Fetherstone and Simons were moved into the main house. It is not known if the two men ever met again but when Fetherstone took his leave a few days later, he and Simons regarded each other as friends, both convinced they had witnessed a supernatural appearance.

Simons was filled with questions. It seemed to him that there were two ghosts, or two halves of the same ghost. The head and torso appeared in the tower bedrooms and some of the corridors inside the old turret. The lower portion of the body was seen downstairs and outside, moving along the avenue of lime trees or in the castle's private graveyard.

One evening, a few days after Fetherstone's departure, Simons was writing letters beside a blazing fire in the drawing room. All at once there was an icy chill in the air and the door burst open on its own accord. Dropping his pen, he ran to the hallway but on finding it empty his gaze was drawn to the window. Beyond the glass pane he saw a breathtakingly beautiful young woman. Only her face was clear, a pale oval among dark tresses which blurred into the night landscape beyond. She looked straight into his eyes, provoking in him both terror and wretched desolation. His hand went to his cheek, wondering if the shapely lips he saw beyond the glass once caressed his skin in a burning kiss.

Who was this tragic young woman and why was her restless spirit haunting Meggernie Castle?

He rode up and down the glen from Brig o' Balgie to Fortingall in the east, to the furthest forester's cottage beyond Loch Lyon in the west. Methodically, gently, he questioned the locals and began fitting together the pieces of a story leading to the gruesome explanation.

Over a century before, when the castle belonged to the Menzies of Culdores, the owner became besotted with a

stunningly beautiful woman. She was many years his junior
and her wit and charm at social gatherings made her the
object of every man's desire. So, when she accepted Menzies'
proposal of marriage he should have been the happiest man
alive. Instead, his joy turned sour, spiralling out of control
into terrible arguments borne of his suspicion and jealousy.
If she so much as smiled at another man, he accused her of
taking a lover and flew into a rage.

One evening, when they retired to their tower bedroom,
Menzies accused his wife of perceived indiscretions with
visitors to the castle. He became incensed by her persistent
denials of infidelity until their argument took a terrible
turn for the worse. In a frenzy of anger, Menzies struck her,
sending her flying backwards to fall and smash her skull on
the bedstead. She was killed instantly.

Whether Menzies felt remorse, no one knows, but he certainly set directly to work to cover up his vile deed.

He seized upon the idea of hiding her body inside a large
chest of drawers. In those days, the chest stood in the alcove
beside the door to the adjoining room. By guttering candlelight, he must have made a closer inspection and realised the
drawers were too small to hold their burden, so he ruthlessly
cut her in half.

When this grisly task was complete, he nailed up the
door to what became Simons' room, locked the door on
Fetherstone's side and then securely locked both of the
rooms so no one could enter from the corridor. As a Chief
of the Clan, Menzies he was a powerful man and knew no
one would challenge any decision he made. He invented
an elaborate story that he and his wife were going away to
visit relatives, adding that they had a notion to sail across to
Europe and take in the sights. He sent all his servants away

with board wages, even his groom, declaring he would take the reins of his carriage himself.

There was nobody to see he was alone when he drove the carriage away, leaving his ghastly hidden secret in the empty castle.

Menzies did not return for several months but when he did, he made himself the object of everyone's sympathy. Tragically, he told them, his beloved wife drowned in a boating accident in Italy.

However, he knew he must remove his late wife's putrefied remains from the chest and decided to bury them in the graveyard. Choosing a dark, moonless night, he swallowed large quantities of whisky to nerve himself for the job. It was horrible, stinking, heavy work and he only succeeded in burying the lower limbs before the dawn began to lighten the eastern sky. He slunk back down the lime walk, exhausted and nauseas.

Back in the tower room, nothing could blank out the stench or touch of the decomposing flesh beneath his fingers. Disgusted, he dropped the body back into the chest's open drawer and stepped back on a loose floorboard and, on exploring beneath the carpet, found it was easily removed. The cavity was a much more convenient grave than trudging down to the cemetery.

He crammed the torso under the floor, slotted the boards back into position and, with a sweep of his foot, the carpet dropped neatly over the top.

Relief must have felt sweet but it was short-lived.

Menzies' body was found the next morning by a servant. The physician reported he was killed with a single deep knife wound to the heart but it is not apparent whether anyone tried to find his killer.

It is clear someone blocked his exit and stabbed him that night, but the locals held their tongues. Theories were whispered and gossiped, believing his killer to have been either his dead wife's ghost or, more likely, her lover or a friend who discovered the truth. It *is* certain, however, the room was not thoroughly searched because her remains were not discovered.

Twenty years after Simons and Fetherstone recorded their experience, Meggernie was purchased by John Bullough, a wealthy cotton machine manufacturer from Accrington. It was then, when extensive renovations were undertaken in the old square tower, that the skeletal remains of a woman were found beneath the bedroom floor. Amid much incredulity, it was confirmed the bones were of only the torso and skull, the lower portion of her body and legs were missing.

Although these mortal remains were laid to rest, right up until 1928 the haunting continued. Even today there are unexplained noises at Meggernie Castle, in the captivatingly wild land of Glen Lyon.

THE CAILLEACH OF GLEN LYON

For time in memoriam, since long before Christianity, there
have been references to the Cailleach.

The name 'Cailleach', meaning hag, does not do justice to
this magnificent female force of Nature. She has been vari-
ously described as a mighty giant of a woman, striding over
mountains and wading thigh-deep across lochs, and also
appearing to mortals through various majestic woman-like
manifestations, to being a haggard old crone. In whatever
guise she appears, she is an enthralling figure, a Mother
Goddess, a protector of all wild creatures and can control the
weather and natural events.

Glen Cailleach is a small glen where the River Cailleach
cuts through moorland between mountains to run down
into Glen Lyon. By their names, the traveller becomes aware
of the local importance of this bleak, windblown landscape.

Hundreds, possibly thousands of years ago the Cailleach
dwelt in this glen. Legend tells us she sought shelter there with
her family, and the locals made her welcome. While she was
there the grass grew sweet and thick, livestock were healthy
and harvests filled the byres every autumn. Huntsmen would
seek her advice before slaughtering deer for their winter pro-
visions and she pointed them to the weak or elderly beasts,
leaving healthy young bucks to thrive for the following year.

For all that she was benign to those who heeded her
words; she was a formidable foe if her land or creatures were
damaged or killed.

The families of the area relied on her astute wisdom of
country lore and she was treated with the utmost respect. To
them, she was regarded as a Deity. By her acute perception
of the ways of the world and life, both mortal and immortal,

she became central to their daily existence. Their food and health depended on her benevolence.

When the time came for the Cailleach to leave the glen, they were thrown into panic.

The Cailleach understood. She gave them custody of four special stones and promised to continue to guard the glen for as long as the people took care of the stones. She instructed them to make a home for the stones so they built a sheiling with a turfed roof on the land beside the river where she once lived. Every year at Bealltainn, 1 May, the stones must be placed outside the sheiling to oversee the glen. Every Samhainn, 31 October, the stones must be placed back inside the sheiling and made secure for the winter.

The first and largest stone, depicting the Cailleach herself, stands eighteen inches high. Its smooth surface was carved over centuries by running water to create a wide bell-shaped base and tapering head.

The second stone is smaller, the Old Man, the Bodach, and then, just a few inches high, their daughter, Nighean.

Ever since then, each of these stones has been placed carefully outside in the dew on the first day of spring. They stand secure, faithfully attended by generation after generation of local country folk. The Cailleach produces another stone in the sheiling every 100 years but these other, smaller stones are left inside the House of the Cailleach, Tigh nam Bodach.

Is this a long-forgotten tradition, lost in this modern age? Not at all.

The Tigh nam Bodach is still nurtured to this day. So, muse on this. What time of the year are you reading this tale? At this moment, is the Cailleach standing among the moorland grass with the wide open sky above her head? Or is she tucked away, dry and safe inside the Tigh nam Bodach?

Go Boldly, Lady

It should be said from the start that this tale is not for the faint hearted.

Hundreds of years ago, a young lady was being wooed by a very handsome man. He would arrive at her father's house accompanied by twelve servants and with his fine horses, immaculate tailoring and the gold on his fingers, his wealth could not be denied.

Her parents found him charming and made it all too clear that they would welcome him as a son-in-law. Their daughter had a wilful personality and with both youth and beauty on her side, she had no wish to be hurried into matrimony. However, it had to be said, her suitor's good looks and wit were very appealing and made her curious to know more about him before agreeing to be his wife.

One day she set off by herself to explore the man's estate and came to a path leading into a wood. She continued on, enjoying the birdsong, glimpses of deer and the sweet scents of wild flowers until she came across a lovely house.

A cage hung beside the front door with a colourful parrot inside.

'Go boldly, lady!' squawked the parrot, 'and don't go boldly, lady!'

She walked into the house and looked around the panelled hallway before opening a door to the first room. A table was laid with sieves presenting piles of oatcakes and cheese. She took some and slipped them into her pocket before moving to the next room.

Here she found racks of beautiful gowns, from thick velvet winter ones trimmed with fur, to thin silks with gauzy petticoats. She smoothed her finger along the satins and silks, lifted lavishly embroidered cuffs and hems to admire the tiny stitches and frothy French lace frills. A chest of drawers drew her eye and, on opening drawer after drawer, she found finger and ear rings, bangles, bracelets and necklaces, all sparkling and shimmering with gemstones and gold.

A smile playing on her lips, she turned the handle on the next door and walked inside.

Pale suspended shapes swung in the draught made by her entrance. They were women's bodies, hanging by their hair from hooks on the ceiling.

Through the chilling fog of shock, she heard the parrot squawk 'Go boldly, lady, don't go boldly, lady,' along with the commotion of people arriving in the hallway. Smothering her screams, she fled to the nearest hiding place: the dogs' kennel.

Who should appear but her suitor with his servants around him. The young lady did not wish to believe her eyes for beside him, laughing and smiling, was her own sweet cousin.

'Young ladies are the better for a drop of blood being drawn,' she heard him say, inviting her cousin to place her feet in a tub of hot water. 'Young ladies are better for a drop of blood being drawn,' he kept repeating.

After what seemed a long time, she heard her cousin say, 'The house is becoming dark …' and then she died.

'May God receive her soul,' one of his twelve servants said, reverently.

The men began to remove the gown and jewellery from the girl's limp, pale body but were unable to pull a ring from her finger. In frustration, the suitor pulled out his sword and sliced off the whole hand, throwing it to the dogs.

The young lady caught it and hid it in the folds of her dress as she crouched at the back of the kennel, placating the barking dogs with cheese and oatcakes. When the men carried the corpse away to hang it up by the hair with the other ladies, she managed to make her escape.

The next day, her suitor called upon her again and this time she agreed to announce their betrothal. She said she would like all her family to be there and organised the seating arrangements so she was between her two male cousins, with her uncle opposite.

When they were all seated, she waited for a moment's calm in the excited conversation.

'I would like to tell you about a dream,' she said clearly, and a hush fell over the company. 'It is nothing more than a dream, mark me well cousins.'

She related everything she witnessed at the house in the woods, adding, from time to time, 'it is nothing but a dream, only a dream.'

Her suitor was growing increasingly anxious with every word she spoke. Nervous glances flickered between his servants standing on the fringes of the room.

All the guests' attention was on the young lady telling her fantastical story, some smiling at its absurdity, others openly disgusted and recoiling, until she came to the part about the hand.

'And if you do not believe me, here is the hand!' she produced her poor cousin's bloodless hand.

Her uncle recognised it to be his daughter's and, within a heartbeat, he and his sons jumped on her murderers.

The suitor and eleven of his servants were hanged, but the court spared the life and set free the servant who prayed for the poor girl's soul when she saw the house grow dark.

THE MAN WITH KNOTS IN HIS HAIR

One warm spring day, a man in Fearnan woke early and seeing blue sky beyond his window, he rose and hurried out to his garden. He worked away, digging and planting, weeding and drawing water from the well to settle his crops firmly in the soil. All was going well until the faeries arrived.

As fast as he dug a hole, they filled it in. He laid down his spade for a moment and it was moved, his trowel was tossed around and played with amid squeals of amusement and the more exasperated he became, the more they teased him.

They chased around him, almost tripping him up every time he went to his shed and troubling him at every turn. He was a mild-mannered man and knew better than to anger the faerie folk but at last his patience broke.

'Och, will ye gie me peace tae work!' he cried. 'Wait until Ah've feenished wi' the gardenin' an' then ye can dae yer wurst tae me!'

When his wife came out to tell him dinner was on the table, she couldn't find him. His spade was in the ground beside the cabbages but there was no sign of her husband. By nightfall, the poor woman was in a sorry state, quite beside herself with worry. She went to her neighbours to say what had happened and they turned out in their dozens to look for him. From old men hobbling along on sticks, to fleet-footed young lads and lassies, they searched the hills, the rivers, waterfalls and glens. There was no sight nor sound of him.

Three days later, the wife was bringing in kindling for the morning fire when her eye caught something unusual in the vegetable patch. Her husband was lying on the soil at the very place he left his spade.

She rushed to his side but her relief turned to panic.

Every strand of hair on his head had a knot tied in it and, as he had a full head of hair, it stood out from his skull like a brush. He couldn't move an arm or leg, nor even raise a finger, but a sound escaped his throat and she leaned in close to hear his words.

He told her he had been in the faerie knoll and seen a great sight: both the good place and the bad.

With a pounding heart, his wife ran for help and they carried him inside to his bed. Advice was sought from a local wise man but he shook his head gravely and said there was nothing to be done: the man would die within forty-eight hours.

Word spread like fire and people came from near and far, clustering around the dying man, seeking answers to many questions. Of those who were taken by the faeries, few people returned so quickly and everyone wanted to know who he had seen. Tearfully, hopefully, they asked after missing relatives and loved ones.

He managed to tell them that only a few people went to the good place. Two days later, he died.

The Loch of the Woman

Overlooking Loch Earn, high on the windswept and rocky foothills of Ben Vorlich, lies Lochan na Mna, 'The Loch of the Woman'. Its remote location and stark appearance begs the question, why would this bleak, inaccessible pool of water be called after a woman? The story behind this name created ripples of hatred, persecution and violence from the clan chiefs right through to the paupers of Strathearn.

It started in the autumn of 1589 when the Keeper of the Royal Forests at Glenartney, near Loch Earn, was instructed to supply venison for a feast. King James VI was bringing Anne of Denmark, his new wife, to Scotland for the first time and all his loyal servants threw themselves into making it a grand celebration.

The Keeper, John Drummond-Ernoch, was proud of his work and knew the red deer would be in peak condition so he could provide the most succulent meat for the table. However, when he went out hunting with his foresters, he found a band of the notorious MacGregors from Balquhidder were already on the hills taking the best of the beasts.

John was furious. Throughout his years of holding the office, he had repeatedly given warnings not to poach the King's deer, and spoken expressly to this local, lawless band of MacGregors. The next day, on coming across the same group hunting in the forest, John and his men chased them down and taught them a lesson. Telling them the time for warnings was over and that his words were obviously falling on deaf ears, he would cut off their ears. Which he promptly did!

For the next week, the King's glens and forests around Glenartney were filled with the sounds of the annual deer rut; stags bellowing and battling for supremacy with great clashing and rattling of antlers. John Drummond-Ernoch rode out with his hunting party and succeeded in fulfilling the requirements for the royal banquets. He took his duties very seriously and felt satisfied he had stopped the poaching and was doing a good job. He enjoyed his privileged position of being in charge of his monarch's vast estate. His domestic life was a happy, comfortable one too, having a staunch friendship with the powerful Stewarts of nearby Ardvorlich Castle, especially since his sister recently married the Laird, Alexander Stewart.

The MacGregors, however, had not been defeated.

Humiliated and physically deformed forever, they may have slunk away to lick their wounds but the pride of the clan was deeply offended. They formed a plan for revenge and bided their time until the focus of their anger, John Drummond-Ernoch, would not have the protection of his friend and ally, the Laird, Alexander Stewart.

One day, word came that Stewart was seen riding out of the glen with the rumour that he would be away for several days. A group of the most bloodthirsty MacGregors set off to track John down during his daily treks on the estate. They soon found him. Alone and taken unawares, he did not stand a chance and was murdered among the pine trees with only his attackers and the wildlife to witness his brutal end. The MacGregors were thrilled by their dreadful deed and chopped off John's head to take away with them, wrapping it in their plaid.

Night was falling when they left the forest and with the moon shining on Loch Earn, Ardvorlich Castle stood out against the shimmering, silver water. Knowing Stewart was away, the idea of visiting the castle was too much of a temptation to resist. It was common knowledge that Stewart's wife was the sister of the man they had just murdered and to take further revenge for their clan's hurt pride, they knocked upon the castle door.

In Scotland, in the sixteenth century, it was customary to give hospitality to anyone coming to your door, providing them with food and drink as a minimum and, if the sun was setting, shelter for the night.

Margaret Stewart greeted the MacGregors with extreme trepidation.

She was vulnerable and unprotected in the gathering darkness, with few servants in the castle and, most importantly, she was very aware of her own delicate condition; her first baby was due imminently.

In the lantern light, the men at her door presented a frightening sight. Their wild hair, stained clothes and the stench of sweat and earth told of heavy days on the hills but, worse, these men were also known rogues and criminals. Margaret, being the Laird's wife, knew their faces and enough of their deeds to feel her heart pounding. She could not turn them away, so she took them into the great hall and invited them to eat the remnants of her own supper: sliced cold shoulder of venison and bread. They scoffed at her, demanding hot food fit for the cold autumn night. It is believed this is the origin of the saying, 'given the cold shoulder.'

Leaving them, Margaret went carefully down the winding stone stairs to the kitchen, holding her candle high to see each step, fearful of slipping and hurting her unborn child. She told the cook to heat something for the men as quickly as possible and the servants jumped to their tasks, terrified to have these dangerous men under the castle roof one minute longer than necessary.

Margaret made her way laboriously back upstairs again and the next thing her servants heard were her hysterical screams. They ran to her aid but the scene was so terrible it stopped them in their tracks.

Grotesquely arranged on a silver salver lay the severed head of John Drummond-Ernoch, Margaret's brother. His mouth was stuffed and spilling over with the bread and meat from Margaret's plate while the MacGregors stood around the table, guffawing with laughter and satisfaction.

Still screaming and choking on sobs, Margaret ran to the castle door, wrenched it open and fled into the darkness.

The MacGregors picked up their grisly trophy, wrapped it up again and left Ardvorlich Castle.

Alexander Stewart returned to his home two days later in a state of grief and great distress. His good friend John was dead and his beloved wife was still missing. Searches were being made across the glen and he had almost given up hope when two young milk maids came to the castle. With breathless urgency, they reported going up on the hills to find a stray cow and seeing a woman lying beside the lochan. John urged them to take him there immediately and they scrambled up the track of a mountain spring until the land levelled out into moorland.

There, desperately weak but alive, lay Margaret, holding her newly born son in her arms.

It is said that Margaret was never the same again. The anguish she must have suffered can only be imagined as she struggled to give birth, alone, on the cold mountain while consumed with grief and shock at the brutal death of her brother. Her son, James Stewart, grew to be a tall, handsome and intelligent man but with a strength and madness about him which many blamed on the traumatic circumstances of his birth.

The MacGregors did not get away with their sins.

The new young chief of the MacGregors of Balquhidder was forced to show his strength and pull the clan together. Whether they condoned the dreadful killing of the Keeper of the Forests or were as disgusted as others, the whole clan were made to pledge to bear equal responsibility. They closed ranks and would not give up the murderers.

For this, and other murderous acts, an edict went out to remove the MacGregor clan from the face of the Earth. For more than 150 years it became illegal to be a MacGregor and the King promised a reward for every MacGregor killed. It was not until 1784 that the beleaguered clan were granted a return of the rights and privileges of an ordinary citizen.

IN THE BLACK WOODS

On a crisp autumn day in 1832, a lone traveller made his way through Glen Lyon. He was enjoying his tour of the area and felt blessed by another fine, sunny day for his adventure. The great mountains rose on either side, folding away into the distance behind him, and ahead, he found new views around every curve of the path winding along the river course. Sometimes, he was close to the River Lyon's rushing waters and would pause to watch the currents rippling around half-submerged stones. Dippers dipped and dived from these sturdy perches, disappearing beneath the water and bobbing up in the flow with a beak full of insects.

By late afternoon, the traveller was wearying. His pace grew slower and the stops to gaze at his spectacular surroundings became more frequent. The previous night he sought shelter in a shepherd's cottage and they told him the glen was very long and sparsely inhabited so he had set out early. With his map in hand, he knew his destination of Bridge of Balgie was still far off but already his own shadow was growing longer and longer, stretching out before him.

There was a frost the night before and the clear sky promised another so he was even more anxious not to sleep beneath the stars. He hastened his pace and after an energetic march up a slope, he stopped to catch his breath and, hands on hips, turned to look up into a patch of woodland. The golden leaves of the chestnut, elm and oak in their full autumnal glory of gleaming reds and burnished copper were well worth his admiration. Dusk was falling rapidly. In no

time, only the mountain peaks were painted with red sun-
light and then, quite suddenly, the light was gone.

He shivered. Was it the chill of dusk or a nasty feeling
of being very small and insignificant in the midst of such
a vast landscape? The hillsides loomed black, towering over
him without features, just huge silhouettes caught in that
indistinct time between day and night.

A noise came from within the wood. A high wail. A child?
A girl crying or calling? He strained to hear.

He had been warned Glen Lyon is one of the Thin Places
of Scotland. Here, the barrier is gossamer thin between this
world and other worlds, allowing phantoms to pass more
freely into our own time and place. He shivered again,
straining to pinpoint the direction of the strange sounds as
he peered up between a lattice of branches and heaps of pale,
collapsing grass and ferns.

The sounds came again; eerie, thin cries and then a low
moan. Remembering this was the last day of October,
Hallowe'en, he shook his head. Witches and ghouls were not
real, he told himself, he must not allow his imagination to
play tricks.

A louder cry forced curiosity to overcome caution and he
stepped off the beaten track and, carefully, quietly, pushed his
way up the hill through tangled undergrowth and overhanging branches. He was holding his breath, avoiding cracking
sticks beneath his boots, all the time chiding himself for the
growing nervous expectation churning in his stomach.

The woodland canopy gave way to a glade where a shaft of
pale moonlight showed a massive cylindrical-shaped boulder in
the centre of the clearing. It was nestled into a pile of rocks with
mosses and lichens smothering the stones' surfaces. Ferns and
saplings poked through the surrounding area of long, dying
grasses and spent summer flowers. It took him several seconds

to take in the scene, narrowing his eyes to try and discern the nature of a dozen or so smooth mounds arranged in a circle around the boulder. Intrigued, he stepped out of the shadows.

A black shape came flying from a tree on the furthest side of the clearing and landed on the top of the boulder. It was a huge black cat. Arching its back, whiskers bristling, it let out a blood-curdling yowl!

The shapes in the grass began to move and the man's screams were lost in a turmoil as the ground seemed to rise up and he found himself in the middle of a growling, hissing mass of wildcats. Their pale green eyes gleamed in the dark, each focused on him as they bared sharp teeth and crept towards him: shoulder blades high, ears flattened back, with their furry bellies low in the grass. He saw with alarm their thick banded tails flicking ominously, while their cries rose louder and wilder into a crescendo.

The large black cat led the cacophony from his lofty stage, stamping his front paws and sheathing and unsheathing his claws. The jagged outline of his jet-black fur shone like silver. His tail was held straight up, swaying slightly with his body but his intense stare never wavered.

All at once, they stopped. Silence. Then they all pounced.

The man took to his heels! Crashing through the trees, falling, scrambling, he lashed out with his arms and kicked with his legs, desperately swiping the cats off where they leapt on him, clinging on with tooth and claw.

At the edge of the trees he was caught by a heavy blow across the shoulders and fell down the bank to roll over and over out onto the open carriageway. Sheer panic gave him the strength to rise and stagger away as fast as he could, zig-zagging with laboured steps, too terrified to look behind him.

Stumbling along under the stars, doubt set in. It was too incredible a scene and the incident passed in such a short time he wondered if it actually happened? Perhaps he fell asleep in the glade and it was just a dreadful nightmare? The black cat on the rock was larger than any he had seen before and the gathering of so many wildcats, surely that could not happen? All the same, it was alarmingly vivid in his mind.

Exhausted, he eventually came to a house and hammered on the door.

The elderly couple who greeted him gasped in shock at the scratched and bloodied state of the wild-eyed traveller. They turned to each other and shared a knowing, fearful look.

'Ye'd best come in,' the man invited, but suddenly shot out a restraining arm, grasping the traveller by the shoulder. 'Wait! Tak yer jaiket off, sir, afore ye step inside.'

The traveller obeyed, fumbling with his belt and buttons and too weak and tearful with relief at finding refuge to query the request.

'Ye've been up at the Black Wood of Chesthill,' the house owner said flatly, stepping forward to help his visitor draw his shaking arms out of the coat sleeves.

'Aye.'

Straining to hold the weight of the jacket, the man held it up, telling his wife to turn the lantern flame up high.

Clinging to the back of the jacket, reaching from the shoulders to well below the hem where his breeches would have strapped above his boots, hung the heavy, striped body of a dead wildcat. Its front legs were spread wide, claws embedded in the tweed, its head tucked close where its teeth still gripped the collar.

Startled and horrified in equal measure, the traveller was helped inside to the fireside where he poured out his tale.

'Sae it's true enough,' the old man nodded to his wife, 'as the legend tells us. The wildcats do come together to worship the Devil Cat at its Stone on the nicht o' Hallowe'en.'

LADY OF LAWERS

There are no records of whether Mary Campbell was any different in character from other children when she was growing up, nor whether she was especially beautiful or clever. However, we do know she was chosen by John Stewart to be his wife and upon their marriage in the early 1600s she moved to Lawers, a small village on the north bank of Loch Tay, beneath Ben Lawers.

From then on she was known as Baintighearn Labhuir, Lady of Lawers, and her rare gift came to the fore, earning her such a remarkable reputation that here we are, 500 years later, still telling her story.

Her husband was a man of means, being the second son of Laird Duncan Stewart 5th of Appin, and her father was Sir James Campbell, Sheriff of Perthshire. Mary enjoyed a privileged if not excessively spoilt life and took her responsibilities as the Laird's wife seriously.

Small though the village was, Lawers was an important ferry port, lying halfway between Killin in the west, Kenmore in the east, and easily reached by boats crossing from the south side of the loch at Ardeonaig.

One day, Mary went down to the waterside to watch the unloading of a consignment of hewn ridge stones to be used to cap the newly constructed village church. When the boat set sail back to Kenmore, she walked up to the church where labourers and craftsmen swarmed over the sturdy structure.

For a few minutes she stood quietly, then announced, 'The ridging stones shall never be placed on the roof of the church.'

The builders smothered their laughter, the more daring calling out, 'My Lady, the stones are a'ready here! And there's plenty hands to lift them aloft!'

By evening a stiff wind was blowing in from the south, raising white crests on the waves and shifting and pulling the loch from shore to shore. The storm reached its peak in the black of night until, exhausting itself with a terrible finale of thrashing branches and crashing waves, it released its grip on the glen under the first grey streaks of dawn.

The neat lines of ridge stones were gone, dragged from the bank and swallowed into the Tay's deep water.

Overnight, the dutiful respect felt by the locals for their Laird's wife grew into awe, and for many, fear. How could she have known such a thing? Was she a witch? Did she conjure up the storm by some mystical force, or was she gifted with the Second Sight?

New capstones were brought in from a different quarry and the church was duly completed. The churned-up patch of muddy ground around it was raked and sown with grass ready for its future as a graveyard. Mary chose to have an ash tree planted close to the building, on the north side. She was surrounded by her family and villagers as she stood beside the gardener filling in the soil around its roots.

'The tree will grow,' she said, 'and when it reaches the height of the gable, the church will split asunder.'

No one laughed or sniggered at this proclamation, nor when she gave two more prophesies connected with the tree. They simply listened to the words of the Lady of Lawers and committed them to memory.

Some years later, the ash tree reached the gable. The community grew uneasy, eyeing the tall, young tree with anticipation and it was not long before their concerns were realised. A raging thunderstorm tore away the slates and smashed the timbers of the west loft of the church, causing months of disruption and repairs. Many believed, however, the real 'splitting asunder' of the church came later when the congregation of Lawers left the Church of Scotland for the Free Church.

And what of Lady Lawers' other two predictions when the ash tree was planted?

'When it reaches the ridge, the House of Balloch will be without an heir.' By 1862, although the church building was now derelict, the strong ash tree was as high as the roof top and, indeed, the Marquis of Breadalbane of the House of Balloch died without an heir.

Her third prophesy about the ash tree was disturbing: 'Evil will come to him who harms the ash tree.'

Her warning must have been forgotten over the passage of time because in 1895 a tenant of Milton Farm, accompanied by a friend, took an axe to the ash tree and felled it.

Shortly afterwards, this farmer was gored to death by his highland bull. His friend was suddenly overcome with an uncontrollable, raving madness and was hauled away to a lunatic asylum and the horse who pulled the cart of ash logs fell down dead in its field.

The Lady of Lawers made many proclamations which have been borne out over time, most, if not all, alarmingly accurate.

'There will be a mill on every stream and a plough on every field,' she said of Lochtayside. It is as if she glimpsed her glen 100 years after her death, when hundreds of ploughs worked the land to produce flax on a huge scale, and the streams pouring into the loch powered more than a dozen mills.

Looking further into the future, did this gifted Seer have a vision of the Clearances when she stated, 'The land will first be sifted and then ridded of its people,' and 'The jaw of the sheep will drive the plough from the ground.'

When Lady Mary was living with her husband and family in the house below Ben Lawers, her neighbours in the glen numbered over 3,500. After the highlanders were forced from their crofts, the parish reported less than 500 souls remaining. This being so, it is true to say her prediction can be confirmed when she said, 'The homes on Lochtayside will be so far apart that a cock will not hear its neighbour crow.'

The Lady of Lawers was the last to own the estate of Campbells of Lawers. She was thrown off the land by the Breadalbanes and it is said she put a curse on their family. Not only did her prophesy concerning the 2nd Marquess of Breadalbane dying without an heir come true, but it came to pass that their estate, which was once one of the biggest in Scotland, was sold off in small parcels to many different owners.

Of her many recorded prophesies, two stand out as being especially disconcerting.

She spoke of seeing 'fire coaches crossing the Pass of Drumochter', yet it was more than 200 years later before the Highland Main Line Railway sent its steam trains powering over the highest point on Britain's entire railway line.

Whether the Lady of Lawers was a witch or not, the accuracy of hindsight has confirmed she was certainly a veritable soothsayer. Perhaps we should take note of one of her predictions which has not yet happened. Or perhaps we should all hope that, for once, she was wrong?

'The time will come when Ben Lawers will become so cold that it will chill and waste the land for seven miles.'

THE MINISTER AND THE FAERIES

Robert Kirk was a very religious man. Born in Aberfoyle to a poor but devout family, he was the seventh son of a minister and from an early age young Robert embraced the scriptures, becoming a clergyman in adulthood.

It is not so much his career or life which has passed into legend, no, it is through his death that Kirk's story lives on by firesides, in inns and through the written word. To appreciate the end, it is useful to understand the beginning, though this tale does not dwell on his many achievements.

Robert was certainly a brilliant scholar, for although his father's stipend would barely cover the needs of this large family, money was found to send Robert to a good school. He then went on to study Theology at St Andrews and later at Edinburgh University. There is no doubt Robert was also compassionate and caring, for there are numerous testimonials of his thoughtful manner towards his parishioners.

So it was, in the latter part of the seventeenth century, that Reverend Robert Kirk took up a position in Balquhidder, in west Perthshire. As a Scots lad growing up in a country parish, he was aware of the tales of faeries, broonies, urisks and all the other unworldly creatures inhabiting Scotland's lochs and glens.

People said he was gifted with the Second Sight due to being the seventh son in the family but whether a Seer or not, this highly educated man of the Church became fascinated by the supernatural world.

Like other men of the cloth during this period, he saw atheists and unbelievers eroding belief in the Christian doctrines of an unseen God and respect for the Father, Son and Holy Ghost. Yet, around him, passed down through generations, he observed a widely held conviction of the Faerie Kingdom.

Robert was a prolific writer; even writing by candlelight through the night to beat a rival, so he could be the first to translate the metrical psalms into Gaelic. In the 1680s such was his standing in the Church that he was called to London to oversee the publication of the Gaelic Bible.

Knowing Kirk's intelligence and astute academic nature, it comes as no surprise to find he started to write a book about Sleagh Maith, or the 'Good People'. Wherever he travelled, he gathered tales of faeries, demons and witches. Disappearances of local people into Faerie knolls, Seers who accurately predicted deaths, fortunes or where a lost loved-one might be found, all were recorded in his neat handwriting to form a growing manuscript.

Shortly after Isobel, his first wife, died, Robert and his little son returned to the parish of Aberfoyle. There he married again, a sweet young woman called Margaret. Throughout this time, his enchantment was growing into a passion for the subject of another ethereal, parallel dimension inhabited by inhuman spirits.

Most evenings he would take a walk up on the Fairy Hill beside the Manse and sometimes he could be seen lying with his head close to the ground, listening for the faerie folk.

One night, he changed into his nightgown and, as was his custom, informed Margaret that he was stepping out to take the air before retiring to bed. Some time passed before Margaret became concerned at his long absence. Ungainly, due to their first baby being due within weeks, she levered herself out of bed and pulled back the curtain to look for him returning.

The garden lay still, bathed in thin grey moonlight. She went downstairs and dispatched one of the servants to search for her husband.

Robert was found lying on Doon Hill, the Fairy Hill, face down: dead.

There was no sign of a struggle or wounds to his body and everyone was perplexed that a healthy man of just forty-seven years of age could just suddenly drop down dead. Eventually, the physician pronounced the cause of death to be the result of a sudden, unexpected fit.

Now, it is well known that faeries do not like their secrets to be told. It is commonly believed the Wee Folk took the minister to their world because of his work prying into their business.

A few days after his untimely demise, on a warm May day in 1692, his loving wife Margaret, his family, friends and the wider congregation gathered at the graveside to witness Reverend Kirk's coffin lowered into the ground. Even during the funeral, there were mourners who doubted the body was that of their clergyman and wondered if they were burying a doppelganger or a box full of stones.

Just a few days later, Robert reappeared in a ghostly form in front of a close relative, proclaiming he was being held against his will by the Faeries. The shocked relative was given precise instructions to follow, which would allow Robert to gain his freedom.

He said that on the day of his new baby's christening, he would appear again and the man was to be sure to have a dagger at the ready. As soon as he saw Robert, he was to throw the dagger over the head of his ghostly image and this would release the spell.

True to his word, Robert *did* manifest himself at this family occasion but unfortunately the poor chap was so knocked for six that, in the precise moment he needed to act, he either froze or simply forgot to throw the dagger.

That was the last time Robert Kirk was seen in this world.

His manuscript lay overlooked for over 100 years. It was not published until it was taken up by Sir Walter Scott in

1815, leading to a further edition with comments by Andrew
Lang in the late eighteen hundreds under the title *The Secret
Commonwealth of Elves, Fauns and Fairies*.

> He heard, he saw, he knew too well
> The secrets of your faerie clan
> You stole him from the haunted dell
> Who never more was seen of man.

(Andrew Lang 1844–1912)

St Fillan's Holy Pool

Some say St Fillan was born in Ireland, others that he was
a Scot from Fife, but all agree he held a rightful place as a
saint. Legend has it that as a baby he was badly deformed
and his father tried to drown him by throwing him into a
lake, but he survived under the care of angels and returned
to be Christened. He became a monk and is understood to
have performed many miracles in his lifetime, and even from
beyond the grave. His death came while in Perthshire, near
Lochearn, causing disagreement as to where to bury such
a fine man. The matter was solved with two coffins, one
interred in Killin, the other at Strathfillan.

The River Fillan holds a healing pool, known as the Saints
Pool or the Holy Pool, where sufferers – whether physically
or mentally affected – could be treated by being immersed
in the river, wich would clear their minds and bodies of their
affliction.

In the late 1700s, a poor Perthshire weaver despaired
when his beloved wife seemed increasingly confused and
angry at the least provocation. Well-meaning folk tried to

help her with the daily tasks but it was soon clear she was losing grip on reality.

Her long brown hair became matted, her skin raw where she scratched in frustration and she spent hours sitting rocking to and fro, staring into space or murmuring and smiling to herself.

A doctor was summoned and a diagnosis declared: the woman had lost her senses and was a lunatic. Distraught, the husband seized upon a friend's suggestion of taking his wife to be cured at the Holy Pool. Here, he was told, the water held special properties bestowed by its connection with the miracles of St Fillan, the seventh-century monk.

The weaver set out on the road to St Fillans with his unkempt wife muttering and dawdling along at his side. On arriving at the village of Tyndrum, close by the River Fillan, he made his introductions to the priest, who spoke briefly with the weaver's wife. The patient's deranged behaviour was all too evident. Her once smooth, pretty face moved rapidly through different emotions without any obvious reason for her change of mood. One moment her features were con-torting with anguish before lighting up incongruously into a beaming smile, her eyes wide under arched brows, a childish laugh escaping her raw, bitten lips.

'The treatment is performed on the first day of each quarter year,' the priest told the anxious man. 'Bring your wife to St Fillan's Chapel just before sunset on that day.'

That year it was a blustery cold evening on the first day of April. A crowd gathered beyond a sharp bend in the River Fillan where a wide stretch of deep, sluggish water formed the Holy Pool. Desperate to have the service carried out, the weaver delivered his wife into the hands of a group of men and women outside the chapel. She struggled and called out pitifully when they restrained her from following him, but he was ushered away and told to return to the chapel for her in the morning.

'All nicht?' he asked, shocked. 'I thocht she was only tae be plunged intae the water?'

'There's mair tae it than that,' he was told, detecting an ominous note in the man's voice.

'Ye'll no' hurt her?' the weaver's heart was beating faster: he should have asked for more details about the cure.

'She'll be back wi' ye in the morn. Now move away, there's others tae see tae.'

Pushing his way through the crowd, the weaver found a tree stump to sit on with a good view of the river and tried to prepare himself for what was to come. Later, he realised, nothing would have prepared him.

When the sun's light drained from the sky, torches were lit. The flames jumped and waved in the wind, filling the air with an acrid scent. A cry went up when a procession appeared from the direction of the chapel with the weaver's wife among its number. Stopping at the water's edge, a stout rope was tied around her waist and despite her wriggling and kicking, she was thrown into the black depths of the pool. As soon as her head appeared above the surface, she was heaved out again.

Dripping and gasping, she laid three stones on the grass before being pulled to her feet and thrown back into the water. This time she was much longer beneath the surface. The circles of ripples completely dispersed, leaving the river flat and mirror-like until with a whoosh, she suddenly surged up, screaming. The crowd shouted and whistled.

The weaver was silent, horrified at the spectacle.

Again she was dragged from the water clutching the stones she took from the riverbed and when these were laid with the others she was thrown into the pool for a third time.

Another cheer went up when she resurfaced. The torch light sparkled off the water streaming from her hair, catching the arcs of spray when she threw back her head, exhausted, clawing her way up the bank on her hands and knees.

No sooner was she on dry land than two of the priest's men helped her to stand, put her gathered stones in her arms and led her to where three cairns rose from the ground. The piles of stones were interwoven with leather halters, tattered lacy nightcaps, gloves, ropes used to lead bulls and all manner of garments. St Fillan's healing powers were called upon for curing animals as well as broken limbs and minds and these offerings were added to the cairns in the ceremonies.

Guided by her helpers, the weaver's wife circled each cairn three times, placing a stone on the cairn at each pass. When all three cairns had received their three stones and her hands were empty, they took her back along the riverside path in the gloaming and up to the ruined chapel.

The weaver ran after them, tears of compassion in his eyes, calling, 'Whur are ye taking her? It's awfy cold and she's drookit!'

'The treatment is nae over yet,' the men called over their shoulders. 'Come back the morn.'

Unable to abandon his wife, he hid behind a gravestone and watched.

First, her hands and feet were bound and she was tied to a wooden frame on top of a large stone, hollowed-out enough to fit a large man into. Then a boy wheeled in a barrow of hay and this was piled over her. Finally, a tall bell, St Fillan's Bell, was placed over her head.

To the weaver's amazement, the men left his wife in this position and walked out of the churchyard to take up guard outside the gates. His wife did not move and made no sound at all.

At first light, the priest walked up to
the chapel accompanied by several
men and women. They removed the
bell from the patient's head, pulled
away the hay and untied her from
the frame. She was pale and calm,
allowing two of the women to
fuss over her, bathing her face,
brushing her hair and smooth-
ing her clothes.

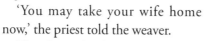

'You may take your wife home
now,' the priest told the weaver.

The clean, docile woman they brought to him was a far
cry from the wretch he handed over the day before and the
young man was profuse in his thanks. Her ordeal must have
been a terrible one but he was grateful to be able to take her
hand again without her snatching it away.

Over the following years he became used to the faraway
look in her eyes and her long silences. She was calm and
managed to keep his house, bearing him three healthy children and setting his food on the table every evening when he
returned from work. However, in his heart he knew this was
not the happy, loving girl he married and chided himself for
asking for miracles.

Hundreds of patients are recorded as being treated at St
Fillan's Holy Pool until a farmer immersed his mad bull and
from that day it lost its powers.

THE SEER OF RANNOCH

On fine summer evenings in Killichonan, Rannoch, Rachel
Cameron enjoyed nothing better than blethering outside

her cottage with her neighbours. A wee burn ran close by and when the sun dipped below the westerly hills and dew dampened the air, clouds of midges would start biting. This natural end to the day forced them to part for the night and retreat inside to prepare their families' meals.

On one such evening they were just rising to go inside when Rachel suddenly looked up and pointed down the road.

'Oh!' she cried out, startled, 'it's a funeral party! Whoever has died?'

Although dusk was falling, it was still light enough for the others to see the road was empty.

'There's no one there, Rachel,' someone said, laying a hand on her arm.

'There! See them, there …'. Rachel's pale blue eyes were wide, watching the procession of figures carrying a coffin between them. 'They're turning into the end cottage,' she whispered, distressed. 'It's Mary's cottage …'

The other women gathered around her. Mary was one of Rachel's closest friends but as they could see nothing unusual about either the road or the cottages, they tried comforting her and persuading her she was mistaken.

Rachel was not listening. Lips parted, her breath coming fast as if she was running, she was completely absorbed in the scene unfolding before her eyes.

'Aw naw!' she shrank back, stifling a sob, 'It *is* Mary! They've wrapped her in her death clothes and are carrying her to the graveyard …'

The graveyard lay beside Rachel's own cottage and with dread etched on her face, Rachel relayed what she was seeing of the phantom procession.

'They're passing us, entering the holy grounds. Now … I hear digging,' her voice cracked with heartbreak, 'a spade slicing into soil, stones scraping the iron, scattering earth.

They are burying Mary.' She swiped at tears streaking down her face. 'I see it so clear ... my dear friend is dead.'

Her friends were scared as much by her chilling words as the look of sheer desolation on Rachel's face.

'Come, Rachel,' one of the older women said, firmly, 'let's all go together to Mary's and we'll show you. Then you'll know she's all richt and I bet she'll have a laugh about you getting yersel' all upset for no reason.'

With false bravado, the party of women walked briskly along the road and tapped on Mary's door.

There was no answer and on letting themselves in, they found Mary sitting upright in her chair: dead.

The old folk were not surprised by Rachel's second sight. It was strong in both her parents' heritage and her mother, a red-haired, vivacious character like her daughter, had been known to have the curse.

Rachel's next vision was so unnerving she could barely bring herself to put it into words.

Her husband, Angus, worked all the daylight hours on his patch of land and running a small mill, returning home for a meal in the middle of the day. That day, Rachel met him at the door, throwing her arms around him.

Clinging to him, shaking, she told of seeing two unearthly figures in the graveyard. Angels, perhaps; one good, one evil. They were raging at each other with a terrible ferocity, trading words and unnerving, guttural sounds with every blow in a formidable battle over who would take the soul of a villager who everybody knew was gravely ill.

All day, shadowy images of people she knew kept appearing before her out of the blue, she told Angus. She knew these people to be alive and well, going about their daily routines, but in her visions their phantoms were carrying out preparations for a burial. On passing the carpenter's shed, although she knew he was away from the village, she heard him sawing and planing wood for the coffin. In the village shop, she saw the likeness of a neighbour choosing material for the shroud, yet she had just passed the same neighbour washing clothes in the burn.

When the old man died, Rachel went around the village clutching her shawl tightly around her despite the heat of the midday sun. With fearful eyes, she watched all these actions being performed again, only this time they were for real. Stumbling back to her cottage, she curled up on her bed, shivering, beads of fever shining on her pale skin.

Word spread of her uncanny ability. Her visions defied logic yet were undeniably confirmed by those who witnessed them. From seeing visions, Rachel's premonitions became more physical. When a family sought her help in finding a lost relative she knew straight away that he was dead and where his body lay. She also felt the agony of his death, suffering the anguish and pain of those final moments.

Waking one morning, she sat bolt upright in bed with a scene flashing before her eyes of a group of men from the west, rushing over the hills towards Rannoch in urgent need of her help. This strong sense of alarm brought scenes of a vast expanse of water whipped up into waves with white crests. She did not recognise the loch or the surrounding hills. Billowing black clouds loomed across the sky shedding torrential rain, and the sound of wind roared in her ears.

In the midst of this disturbing sight she saw a man battling for his life on a little sailing boat as he made a desperate bid to reach the shore, but the storm was too strong. Suddenly, she was caught up in the sailor's panic, feeling the boat capsize beneath his feet, tasting the foul, suffocating water dragging him down with the wreck.

Left breathless and weak from her vision, Rachel lay back on her pillow and ran her fingers reassuringly over the familiar blankets. Slowly, her heart stopped its wild thumping and she calmed herself down. Then, she rose from her bed, prepared food for her large family, kissed her beloved Angus before he left for the mill and settled to wait for the expected visitors.

Within the hour, the victim's family were knocking at her door, having travelled for days from Loch Awe. Before they had a chance to speak, Rachel blurted out all they needed to know.

These incidents brought attention to Rachel's quiet community of Killichonan. Reverend J Sinclair, renowned for his interest in all things supernatural, came to see her and recorded the details. In turn, Sinclair's reports reached London, bringing Lord Bute to the remote glen in 1895 in his capacity as Vice President of the Psychical Research Society.

Second sight, or da shealladh, can be considered a gift or a curse, but unfortunately for Rachel, painful and terrifying as it can be, a Seer has no choice but to live with it.

THE LAIRD'S BET

Near Rannoch there lived a Laird who, it was said, dabbled in the black arts for amusement. He was an ebullient fellow who meant no harm yet enjoyed nothing better than playing tricks and jokes on his friends.

Each year this Laird held a grand ceilidh which everyone on the estate looked forward to and attended. One year he decided to liven up the usual gathering of dancing and drinking by declaring all the guests must take part in the games he devised. What was more, he would give a golden guinea to the best entertainer in each of his events, such as who was best at singing a song, telling a story, or showing off a unique ability.

The ale and whisky flowed and the evening progressed with much music and laughter. A skinny little scullery maid with the voice of an angel won herself a guinea by charming her audience with a fine ballad. A stout young boot boy outshone the other lads by walking effortlessly on his hands and performing cartwheels, back rolls and great leaps down the length of the long barn.

Standing quietly at the side was Sandy, the Laird's slow-witted cattleman. Each time his turn came to sing or perform in some way, he hung his head and shyly refused.

When the Laird's next competition was to tell the biggest lie, he called out to Sandy to take part or leave. Sandy looked at his feet and rubbed his chin but was unable to think of a lie so the Laird sent him out to clean his boat.

The sky was darkening into night when Sandy plodded forlornly down to the lochside. The distant strains of fiddle music and cheerful voices made his solitude even more intense and he felt sad to be sent away. He collected a scrubbing brush and bucket from the boat shed and climbed into the boat.

With a lurch, the bow of the boat rose up and it sped forward, breaking from its moorings and racing across the water. Easily confused and bewildered at the best of times, poor Sandy was stunned. Eventually, the fierce wind whipping against his face forced him from his daze and he gripped the seat and clung on for dear life.

Looking down to take a better grasp, he couldn't believe what he saw. His feet were dainty, clad in green silken slippers, his legs were slender and covered with silk stockings showing below a fine taffeta gown. As the boat slowed, approaching the furthest shore, he smoothed his hands over his chest feeling a woman's body beneath his fingers and on tentatively peeking over the side of the boat he saw the reflection of a beautiful woman.

The boat swept smoothly through the shallows and came to rest on a grassy bank, where Sandy alighted. No sooner had he inspected himself again in a state of bemusement, than a handsome young man came along the shore.

The man was immediately attentive, hurrying to the side of this lovely young woman to ask if she was all right and if he could be of service.

Sandy's silence was taken as coyness and when asked his name Sandy knew he could not reply 'Sandy the cattleman', so he murmured, in his new girlish tones, that he could not recall.

Concerned, and believing the young lady must have lost her memory in distress, the man politely escorted her to his mother's house. As the weeks passed, the young man fell in love with the beguiling girl he found wandering alone by the water.

Sandy the cattleman was no more. Transformed completely into this new female image, she returned his feelings, finding herself loved and happier than ever before. They were married and created a warm, comfortable home together which, in due course, produced two delightful children.

One evening the couple took a walk by the lochside and came across the Laird's old boat. Having been abandoned long ago when Sandy first arrived, it was covered with moss and pooled with dead leaves and stagnant water. She stepped in to clean it and, instantly, it shot away from the bank, carrying her back across the loch.

Crying and shrieking in anguish, Sandy screamed to the heavens to stop the boat and take her home to her husband and children. The boat careered onwards. With a long, heart-rending howl, Sandy knew she was changing. Gone were her feminine clothes, slippers and smooth skinned, fine boned arms and wrists, replaced by muscular forearms, moleskin breeches and big cow-pat-stained boots.

When the boat came to a rest at its moorings on the Laird's land, Sandy the cowman stumbled onto the bank and made his way towards his old lodgings at the farm. On passing the big barn he heard sounds of merriment and saw the Laird at the door waving and calling to him.

'Whatever's wrong, Sandy?' the Laird inquired, drawing the distraught figure into the ceilidh. 'You are upset? Tell us what happened.'

Sandy could not tell a lie so he related how he was taken across the loch by the boat, changed into a beautiful woman and married a kind, fine-looking man. With tears streaming down his cheeks, he described the house they lived in and their two sweet children.

'My goodness, Sandy!' the Laird roared with laughter. 'We are still playing the game of telling the best lie and that is definitely the biggest lie we have heard! You have won a golden guinea!'

Indeed, only twenty minutes had passed since Sandy was sent away from the party to clean the boat but the Laird had employed his dark arts and mesmerised him.

Yellow-Haired William

Another tale not for the faint of heart – a man from Clan MacGregor was discovered to have committed terrible deeds.

What these deeds were, we have no knowledge, but the penalty for his acts was death. He was captured and brought before the clan chiefs, who told him his life would be spared if he carried out a particular task. He was instructed to bring them seven heads; but all must be of yellow-haired men – tricky in an area of dark haired people.

MacGregor seized the chance to save his own life and set off on horseback to scour the land for hapless victims. He carried with him a large saddlebag and soon it was heavy with six heads, but the seventh eluded him.

Riding through Glen Fender, he spotted a young man tending his animals high up on the Meall Dail Min. The herdsman was young, strong and as fit as a flea, a formidable opponent if challenged to a fight. This would be no easy prey but the shining crown of sun-bleached, golden hair caused the cowardly murderer to rein in his horse.

MacGregor began by engaging the lad in a shouted conversation, asking directions and complimenting him on his fine highland cattle.

Young William met few people during his long hours of work and was pleased to break his lonely vigil. Oblivious to any danger, he wandered down towards the friendly horseman to hear his words more easily.

Dismounting, and tying his horse in the shade of a tree, MacGregor ambled casually up the path. He needed to keep the herdsman a distance away from the stomach churning odour of rotting flesh coming from the grisly cargo bulging in the bag behind his saddle. Judging the air to be clear, MacGregor sat down on a nearby boulder and invited William to join him in taking snuff. The young man was happy to accept.

They sat together in a companionable manner until William was taking the snuff. In a trice, MacGregor pulled out his sword and cut off his head.

The headless corpse toppled forward and rolled a few yards down the track and that is where it was found. To this day Carn Uilleam Buidle, 'Yellow William's Cairn', stands on the spot in memory of William, the young herdsman from Ardcampsie.

No doubt thrilled to have secured his last fair-haired victim, MacGregor placed the head in his large leather bag. He stayed at the Little Lude Barn that night and local men told of seeing a stranger there and glimpsing the bloody trophies. Forever after, the barn has been called Sabhal nan Seachd Cinn, the 'Barn of the Seven Heads'.

Wee Iain MacAndrew

Iain MacAndrew was a short, skinny man with a huge reputation.

Known throughout his life as Wee Iain MacAndrew of the Arrows, he possessed a skill with his bow and arrow which no man could equal, let alone surpass. This ability brought him fame throughout the region and made him a very useful ally to those in need of protection. However, MacAndrew could just as easily use his talents for nefarious pursuits and held no qualms about killing either man or beast.

One time he rode off with catarans to steal stock in the Lochaber area. Anyone foolhardy enough to stand in their way was quickly dispatched by one of MacAndrew's arrows. Their wild foray in the west left chaos and heart-break in its wake. Crofts and villages were robbed, valuable winter stores plundered from barns, and heifers, sheep and pigs were gathered up and herded away to sell on their journey home.

The Lochaber men were in uproar at the savage raid. They soon discovered the bowman responsible for killing their friends and brothers was the notorious Wee Iain MacAndrew of the the Arrows. After burying their dead, they set off to seek revenge.

A week or so after returning from Lochaber, Wee Iain was sitting at his own hearth turning bannocks on the girdle. He may have been ransacking and causing carnage while away in the glens beyond Rannoch Moor, but it was a different matter at home. His plump, big-boned wife ruled the house. No doubt there was a gentle side to the woman, though few saw it, but she was a fine match for him and kept an orderly, well fed house by way of her sharp tongue and common sense.

While Iain watched the scones did not burn, his wife was busy at the table preparing another batch of baking.

The clamour of horses and deep voices heralded the appearance of several men at the door. Mrs MacAndrew met them with an annoyed expression, her flour-covered hands showing she did not like to be interrupted in the middle of her chores. They asked if she knew where Wee Iain MacAndrew of the Arrows was and she nodded, inviting them in and saying he was not far away.

There were twelve men in all and as they clustered into the parlour, Mrs MacAndrew picked a freshly baked bannock from the table and tossed it towards her husband.

'These men are efter yer Master, away and find him and tell him tae come hame.'

Wee Iain took a bite from the warm scone and scurried out the front door. As soon as he was out of sight, he bent low to scamper, unseen, behind the bushes and tethered horses, circling round to the back of his cottage.

'Help yersels tae bannocks,' his wife thrust the tempting tray towards them 'I ha'e some beer somewhere, I'll fetch it fer ye.'

She went through to the back closet and quickly opened a shuttered cupboard beneath the window where Iain stored his bow and arrows. Then, taking care not to make a sound, she opened the window shutters and passed the quiver and arrows out to her waiting husband.

While his wife kept the men's attention indoors, Wee Iain climbed the tallest tree in front of his house; a climb he'd made many a time before.

The ale drunk and the baking devoured, Mrs MacAndrew suggested her husband should be home any minute and perhaps someone would be able to see him coming if they took a look up the glen.

One of the men strolled to the open door and stepped out, but he did not return to say if their prey was in sight. After a few minutes, another man decided to check what was happening and left the parlour. He, too, did not return. Then another took his pistol in hand and ventured out, and another, until all twelve men left the house.

Mrs MacAndrew followed the last man to the doorway. She paused to wipe her hands on her apron and listen for any sounds, then stepped out into the fresh daylight.

All twelve men from Lochaber lay dead, sprawled on the grass on either side of the cottage. Each one killed swiftly by Wee Iain's flying arrows before they even had a chance to cry out or return to tell their tale. And that is how Wee Iain MacAndrew became a legend in his own time.

MOVING NORTH

The Whistler

Paul was just a lad when he first became aware of the spirit shepherd of Glen Tilt.

It was autumn, with frost prickling his nose and numbing his fingers, but he was keen to go up the glen with his father to bring the sheep off the hill. Threatening snow clouds smothered the high peaks of Beinn a' Ghlò as the woolly mass obediently wound their way down to the lower slopes. Then a ewe split from the others and struck off towards a dangerous rocky outcrop.

At first Paul thought the whistling he heard came from wind whipping through the heather and boulders but it came in short blasts: shrill, commanding. Further up the hill, the ewe suddenly stopped, her head jerking round as if caught by an invisible crook before swinging round and scampering back to join the flock.

'That's the Whistler at work,' his father told him, a look of wonderment in his eyes. 'You never see him, but you hear him, as you did just now, didn't you? He's not to be feared, Paul, he takes care of the sheep.'

As the years rolled by Paul stepped into his father's shoes to tend the sheep. In summer months he explored every nook and cranny of their patch of the long glen running between the massive bulk of Beinn a' Ghlò on the northern skyline and Blair Atholl in the south.

On swelteringly hot days he would lie back among the butterflies and wild thyme, squinting up into fathomless blue sky where larks sang and eagles soared. During dark, snowy winters he and the other shepherds would gather their sheep into folds and huddle down in the lee of the stone walls.

They were all aware when the Whistler was nearby. His presence could be detected by characteristic whistles and the sheep were quieter, more settled. Sometimes the spirit shepherd spoke to them as clearly as if by words from a mortal's mouth. 'Leave the sheep, they are safe with me,' he would say.

One day, when the River Tilt was bubbling and roaring in spate, Paul and fellow shepherds were out in the rain-soaked dusk. They were keeping a watchful eye in case their animals ventured too close to the rushing water.

'Ah doubt the Whistler will no' be wi' us the nicht,' one man said, peering into the gloom.

The spirit's response came immediately, 'I created the spirit laws. I went round by the bridge and here I am.'

Sometimes the Whistler would call to Paul when he was out on the hills, 'Leave the sheep, Paul!' and Paul would set off south towards the farm to do essential chores. He trusted the spirit shepherd.

Hungry foxes and wildcats were not the only dangers to the flock– thieves roamed the glen. There were plenty of wooded areas to hide out in and a ready supply of the Duke of Atholl's fish and game to eat or sell. A sheep, however, made a fine prize and could garner a healthy price at market.

One day, when Paul ached from neck to knee from chopping logs, he plodded up the valley for his nightly vigil.

'Leave the sheep, Paul!' the Whistler shouted to him, 'Leave the sheep!'

Gratefully, Paul turned on his heel and retraced his steps with his mind on the beckoning comfort of a dram, his mattress and a deep sleep.

That night a thief was watching Paul's flock from the edge of a copse. Under the shifting light of clouds cloaking a gibbous moon, he smiled to himself; the sheep were unattended. Skulking across open pasture to crouch behind low bushes and rocks, he got close enough to pounce on one of Paul's grey sheep. It jumped forward in panic but with ill-gotten skill the thief soon wrestled it to the ground, binding its front and back feet together with canvas garters.

After a quick glance over his shoulder to see the coast was clear, he heaved the sheep onto his back.

Suddenly, the Whistler struck a forceful blow, shouting, 'Leave the sheep!'

The robber was sent sprawling to the ground, the sheep flung off in the opposite direction. Swiping a hand over his eyes, he looked up for his attacker, bracing himself for a fight. To his surprise the hillside was empty, the night air silent except for the plaintive bleats from the poor beast struggling in the grass a few yards away.

There was nobody there.

A terrible fear engulfed him. Digging his heels into the damp pasture and shuffling backwards, he frantically peered around him. Who hit him? His ears were ringing from the blow yet he was sure he heard a voice telling him to 'leave the sheep'. Scrambling to his feet, he ran away as fast as his hammering heart and airless lungs could carry him.

Early the next morning,
Paul went up the glen with
two other shepherds and
they found a strange sight awaiting
them. At first glance, the flock appeared to
be safe and well but on drawing closer Paul saw a
ewe lying apart from the others. He hurried to her side
and dropped to his knees.

'Her feet are bound,' he murmured.

'That's the way of the thieves,' one man said, helping to
untie the binding.

'Why didn't they take her?' the other asked.

'The Whistler was looking after them,' Paul told him, 'the
Whistler kept them safe.'

TAM MACNEISH

Tam MacNeish was a quiet, unassuming man in early middle
age. His business was sufficiently successful to provide a
house, two servants and a good horse. While Tam was perfectly happy with the way his life was going, his family, and
especially his mother, urged him to find a wife.

Tam ignored or politely turned down invitations to func-
tions where local young ladies might be presented to him,
choosing to spend his free time reading or walking up into
the hills for a bit of shooting.

After a pleasant afternoon potting a rabbit and a couple of
grouse for the larder, he was heading home under a clear blue
sky when he noticed a pool of mist rising from woodland on
the horizon.

He stopped, watching it form into a denser cloud and
speed towards him. There was no wind to carry this cloud,

no reason he could see for it having formed and he immediately felt uneasy. Reaching for his gun for protection, he
knew a bullet would have no effect on an evil presence so he
placed a silver sixpence in the gun and fired.

The circlet of fog evaporated with a scream of agony!

A figure dropped to the hillside, thudding into the tus-
socks of heather and rolling over and over to come to rest in
a hollow. Slipping and sliding, Tam rushed down the steep
slope and fell to his knees beside a young woman in a dishev-
elled state. She was clothed only in a light cotton nightdress
and blood seeped through the pale material wrapped and
tangled around her thighs. Regardless of decorum, Tam
pulled the material aside to discover a deep graze scored
across both her legs from where the sixpence passed.

Although awake, the woman did not reply to his questions. Was she in pain? Could she walk? What was her name?
She moaned a little, her wide blue eyes white-ringed with
panic but otherwise she was silent.

Tam was full of remorse. He picked her up and carried her
home, ordering the housemaid to bring bandages and water
to tend to the woman's injuries.

On hearing what had happened and how she fell from a
cloud, the housemaid crossed herself furiously and refused to
have anything to do with the patient.

'She's from the faeries' world,' she cried, gawping at the
woman lying on the bed. 'Take her back up there! She might
be a witch or a changeling! Master, you should not have
brought her here.'

His family and friends told him the same: take her back to
where he found her, she was not of their world and no good
would come of having her under his roof.

Tam was too consumed with regret at having wounded
the poor young woman to abandon her while she was so

badly injured. Instead, he nursed her himself. When the wounds healed, she followed him around the house and he set her to work in the kitchen. The housemaid was petrified and refused to return until he banished 'yon weird woman' from his house. To Tam's surprise, his patient took up all the chores the maid had done and within a few days he saw his home cleaner, his meals tastier and his clothes mended and cared for better than ever before.

There was something very disturbing about the woman, though, and it gnawed away at him. Where had she come from and why did she never speak?

He consulted a friend who had an interest in the workings of the faerie underworld. His friend was curious and came to meet the woman then suggested Tam should return to the very spot he first saw her, exactly a year to the day of the shooting.

'Wait where you stood at the moment you shot her, look around, listen to the sounds beyond the larks and the breeze in the heather. Perhaps you will learn more about your maid.'

So Tam took himself up the hill on the anniversary of the incident and sat down to observe anything and everything. Nothing happened. He ate the cheese and apple, drank some water from a nearby stream and, not wishing to use his gun, counted dozens of missed opportunities to shoot something for his table. Still, nothing happened.

As the sun dipped low, he heard a noise higher up the hill. A light showed briefly, disappeared, then showed again. He crept closer and saw a hole in the ground large enough for a man to walk through and, beyond the entrance, a crowd was gathered in a cave.

Nearest the door, a man was presiding over the company, calling for quiet. He held up a cup, saying, 'A year ago I was waiting for my bride. She did not come to me! I may never see her but, I tell you, I have placed a spell on her so she will never speak again ... unless she drinks from my cup!'

The crowd cheered and laughed, raising their drinks in a toast.

Tam ran forward into the mouth of the cave and the merriment changed in an instant to shouts of alarm, jeering and demands for him to leave.

'I shall go as soon as I may have a drink, as you have all been enjoying!'

All eyes turned to the man who proposed the toast. A hush followed as he dipped his cup in the bowl of punch and handed it to Tam.

No sooner had his fingers closed around it than Tam threw the contents on the ground, pocketed the cup and ran helter-skelter down the hill and along the track to his house. He did not stop until he was inside his own front door, terrified by what he witnessed and disbelieving of his own courage.

When he was calmer, he washed the cup, filled it with milk and took it to the woman, insisting that she drink. She refused, shaking her head and edging away from him. He tried again and again but she would not take the cup so he went to where his sword hung over the hearth and told her he would drive the sword through her heart if she did not drink.

The woman drank the milk from the cup. Then she looked up at Tam and with tears swimming in her eyes she coughed and cleared her throat, crying out, 'Oh, thank you! Thank you! I can speak again!'

Now she could answer his questions and they sat talking together by the fireside until the clock struck midnight.

The woman, whose name was Ishbel, recalled her life in the city of Edinburgh where she worked in a hotel. It was a good hotel, run by the man who became her husband, but all memories stopped after the moment she fell asleep on her wedding night.

Tam had never been to Edinburgh but the very next morning he and Ishbel set out for the city which she knew as home. She guided him straight to the hotel and, telling her to conceal her face with her shawl, they entered by the tradesmen's entrance and asked for food in the kitchens.

The servants were exasperated, telling them it was a bad day to ask for charity for they were all at their wits' end about their Mistress.

'She's dying! A full year she's been lying like a corpse and the doc's just told the Maister he cannae dae anither thing fur her. Oor poor Maister, he's a1' in bits aboot it!'

'I am a physician,' Tam said boldly. 'Tell your master I will take a look at your Mistress.'

The distraught Master of the house received Tam with a pessimistic grimace and weak handshake.

'Well sir, I doubt you'll do any harm, so I will accept your offer to attend my wife's bedside.'

The woman laid in the bed was turned away, facing the wall. Tam walked round the room and tried to see her features and raise a response. Apart from whining that she could not turn over on the mattress, she looked like a corpse.

'Sir, please leave us alone,' Tam said with authority, ushering the husband out the door.

As soon as they were alone, he ordered the creature to sit up. She did not move. He raised his voice and demanded that she sit up and get out of bed. When there was no response he drew out a dagger and swore he would drive the blade through her heart if she did not get off the bed!

With the thrumming noise of a hive of bees, the body rose from the bed and shattered into a thousand pieces, swarming up to the ceiling in a buzzing mass where it burst into flames. Tam ducked low, covering his head with his hands as the blazing ball whirled round the room and shot out the window.

The bedroom door burst open and the husband stared aghast at the empty bed.

'Have no fear,' Tam gave him a reassuring pat on the shoulder, 'your wife is safe and well. The faeries removed her on your wedding night and made a poor copy to leave in her place. It was empty of soul, a mere living corpse. Come down to the kitchen with me ...'

Dazed and confused, the man obediently followed Tam down the stairs.

Ishbel was waiting in the scullery and on seeing her husband, she leapt to her feet and ran to him, pulling her shawl away so he could see her face.

Tam was pleased to have reunited the young couple and stayed a few days with them to celebrate. Then he returned home, re-engaged the housemaid and looked forward to spending his days reading books or walking the hills. As far as looking for a wife was concerned, he decided life was much easier without one.

The Woman who Lived with the Deer

In the days when Scotland was ruled by the Stuarts and no man could move faster than the speed of a galloping horse, a little girl wandered from her croft and was lost on the mountains around Blair Atholl.

Her frantic parents ran to their neighbours to plead for help to find their daughter. Old and young, they turned out to search, calling her name, peering among thickets, climbing up onto the highest slopes and shouting down into waterfall-soaked ravines. Their quest spread over days, then weeks, then months.

'The faeries ha'e taken the bairn,' the old folk decided. Such a bonnie wee lass would be looked on kindly in their world and maybe, one day, she would be returned to her mother's arms. The girl's parents tried to take comfort from these words but in every waking hour they were blighted by the pain of unremitting loss. Somehow, they summoned the will to rise each day to tend their land and beasts but their eyes were always straining to see a movement on the hills, their ears pricked for the slightest sound which might be from a child.

Some years later, a traveller passed their door and it being near sunset they offered him shelter for the night. Sharing their porridge by the fire that evening, he told them tales of his journey and of a strange sight he came across a few days earlier.

He was walking due east as the sun was rising, admiring the fine red glow to the sky and the mist hanging over the river in a veil down the glen. At the edge of a wood, he came across a herd of deer. The does were lying in the grass or grazing with long-legged fawns at their sides. Several young bucks wandered between them and a nine-point stag snatched mouthfuls of the heather, occasionally stopping to scratch at his ear with a raised hind hoof.

It was a very peaceful scene and the traveller had no wish to disturb the herd so he leaned against a pine tree to watch the blood red ball of the sun explode over the horizon.

In the growing daylight, he came to notice a figure lying with the deer.

'It was lying with its head against the belly of a hind, cooried in, an arm resting on the animal's foreleg. My eyes were drawn to it when it sat up. It stretched its arms above its head and yawned and I saw this was a lass! Her face was oval with large, dark eyes … an enchanting face. All else about her was wild! When she stood up she had no clothes, none at all! I admit to noticing she was young and slender but little of her body was left uncovered because of her cascading, untamed hair.'

The couple leaned eagerly towards their visitor. 'Where did you see her? Where? Our daughter has been missing for fifteen years … perhaps it is her!'

The next day the father set out with two friends on the long walk in search of the herd in the neighbouring glen. When darkness fell and there had been no success, they slept in a shepherd's bothy. This continued for days until they met a woodsman and told him their task.

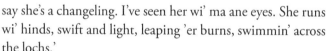

'Oh aye, the wild woman who lives wi' the deer? Some say she's a changeling. I've seen her wi' ma ane eyes. She runs wi' hinds, swift and light, leaping 'er burns, swimmin' across the lochs.'

'D'ye ken where we'll find her?'

'Aye, I'll tak ye there the morrow.'

They found the red deer resting in a mossy glade beside a lochan. The big russet-brown beasts lay still, disguised by dappled sunshine filtering through the canopy of thickly leaved oak and elm. The girl was with them, kneeling in the shallow water. Using both hands to hold back her mane of moss entangled hair, she lowered her face towards its cool surface and took a long drink.

One glance at the figure and her clear profile was enough for the father to recognise the resemblance to his wife's features. He called out to her.

Instantly, the herd jumped in alarm and took to their heels, the girl keeping pace with them, her hair whipping around her body like hundreds of fine ropes.

It took several days but eventually they caught her and took her home. She did not struggle or cry and if she did not understand the men's words, she understood well enough they felt only love and kindness towards her.

This lost little girl who was raised with the deer slowly responded to the comforting, dimly recalled familiarity of her mother and father in the thatched cottage. Cared for and loved as she was by her human family, if the red deer were grazing in the glen she gazed at them with an anxious expression of yearning, whispering, 'my beloveds, my beloveds …'

A Devilish Card Game

Many years ago, when Loch Treig Head was a bustling marketplace for drovers from miles around, the menfolk would meet at the inn for a blether and a game of cards. Its remote setting meant it was unusual to see members of the gentry so it caused a stir when, one frosty evening, a stranger stepped through the door.

It was late and most of the locals had gone home to bed but he was greeted by stares from the innkeeper and three men hunched over a table playing cards by the hearth. He was a good-looking fellow: tall and broad shouldered, exuding confidence in every movement. With his big smile of gleaming white teeth, black hair falling in waves to his shoulders, gold rings on his fingers and a colourful embroidered waistcoat glimpsed beneath his cloak: this was a man of means.

The shepherds invited him to join them by the fireside, dragging an extra chair to their table and offering the seat closest to the warmth of the flames. The stranger thanked them and asked the landlord to bring over a large jug of ale for them all to share. He was excellent company! They listened, enthralled, while he regaled them with tales of his exploits abroad on the Continent, incidents in the houses of lords and dukes across Scotland, anecdotes of meeting royalty and even boasting of his conquests with beautiful women from Rome to Inverness.

The local men, friends since childhood, were having a grand evening. The beer flowed and the card games sped along. The only slightly irksome thing was that the stranger was winning every game. Knowing they were already in trouble with their wives due to the late hour, they murmured excuses to leave.

The stranger laughed, telling them not to worry about their wives' sharp tongues. Were they not the men of the house, should they not stay as long as they wished?

All three knew it was a bad idea to upset their womenfolk and exchanged anxious glances, but not one wished to voice their concern in front of this worldly gentleman. At the end of the next game, one of the shepherds declared he would really have to go or it would be dawn before his eyes closed, which would never do because he had a busy day ahead. His friends echoed these words and they too decided to call it a night.

'Before we part,' the stranger asked, 'can I tempt you to a game using my cards?' He turned his charming smile to each in turn. 'Here,' he drew a pack of cards from an inner pocket and shuffled them with skilful fingers, ending with an exuberant flourish to spread them out, face up, in an arc on the table.

'These cards are different,' the stranger said, his eyes sparkling beneath his long, black lashes. 'They tell of the future; your desires, hopes and fortunes.'

The cards were indeed different, quite unlike anything the men had seen before. Lavishly illustrated in coloured inks, they depicted figures in different poses and garbs, surrounded by intricate entwining leaves and calligraphy. They were a far cry from the shepherds' own deck purchased from a packman at the market.

They settled back down into their seats, intrigued.

'These are Tarot cards.' The gentleman shook back his raven mane, poised his hands above the table for a second then gathered the cards together in a theatrical sweep of his hand before presenting them to one of the shepherds. 'Please, shuffle them yourself. Then place the pack on the table, face down.'

When this was done, he was instructed to cut the pack and turn over the chosen card.

The shepherd did as he was bid to reveal a card showing a Jester grinning foolishly.

'Ah!' the stranger cried. 'You, my friend, make silly mistakes and should take heed of this warning.'

The next shepherd shuffled the cards very thoroughly before making his cut: a picture of a blind-folded man.

'Well, this is clear to see …' the stranger looked knowingly at the shepherd, 'you must open your eyes to the world!'

When it came to the third shepherd, he was full of trepidation. Cautiously, he turned over the chosen card and stared at it with eyes widening in horror: a smiling picture of Death.

Trembling with shock, the man dropped the card and it fell to the floor, floating slightly towards the fire as it caught the updraft. The shepherd lunged for it, falling out of his seat and landing, kneeling, on the floor under the table.

The card lay beside the stranger's feet but they were not feet … they were iron clad hooves.

'Run lads!' he yelled, leaping up, knocking over his chair and bounding towards the door. 'It's the very De'il Himself!'

His friends jumped up and fled after him, wrenching open the door and dashing out into the night. The dark stranger came hard on their heels! As they rushed through the freezing air, their ears were filled with the dreadful sound of his cloven hooves clanging and clattering over rocks, the iron shoes sending up sprays of sparks to add to their panic every time they dared to snatch a glance over their shoulders.

The shepherds made it to the safety of their homes, slamming home the bolts on their doors and breathlessly relating their ordeal to their astonished wives.

It is said they last glimpsed the Devil racing up Lairig Leacach in great bounds, his cloak floating out behind him. If you look carefully on the rocks around Loch Treig House,

now called Creaguaineach Lodge, you may see the Devil's hoof marks from that fateful night.

The Witch and the Shepherd

When she heard the news, the witch leapt up and danced a jig of jubilation! A boat had sunk crossing the straits to Skye between Glenelg and Kyle Rhea and there were no survivors. She knew one of the passengers on the little vessel and his death meant she was a step closer to claiming a valuable inheritance.

Losing no time to remove the only remaining obstacle, she threw a cloak around her shoulders and hurried along the tracks and over moorland up to Glen Loch. Her feet barely touched the sodden earth as she raced along, cloak billowing,

The shepherd tending his sheep in Glen Loch was unaware of the imminent danger. His mind was on his flock in the driving rain and low cloud; it was a very wet day to be out on the hills. So cold he could no longer feel his fingertips, he gathered the sheep into a fold and, calling his dogs to heel, sought shelter in the bothy at Ruigh Chuilein.

The witch was watching him and nipped in through the door before he dropped the latch.

The collies bared their teeth and snarled, lying low on the smooth mud floor, ready to pounce.

'Tie up your dogs!' the witch demanded.

The shepherd looked at her, askance, sensing her evil intent.

'I have nothing to tie them with,' he shrugged, making an effort to pull the dogs to the far side of the hut.

The witch pushed her hood away and tugged two long dark hairs from her own head. 'Tie them up with these!'

The shepherd took the hairs and tied them around a beam on the wall, pretending to secure the other ends around the dogs' necks while telling the dogs to sit still.

'Now,' the witch stalked back and forth in front of the empty hearth, relaxed in her belief the dogs were tied up, 'we need to talk, you and I. I have news of the owner of the pastures in Glen Girnaig. He has drowned on his trip to Skye. As you well know, that land will now become yours and on your death, it will be mine …' She held his gaze with a steely stare. 'We need to reach an agreement for I do not wish to wait for time to run its course.'

The shepherd was aghast. The victim of the drowning was well known to him and he was deeply shocked to hear of the accident. More pressing, however, was how to deal with the malicious crone prancing around in front of him.

'Are you listening?' she hissed, her temper rising. 'You are all that lies between me and the fertile green land I should rightfully own!'

When the shepherd did not respond, she leapt towards him, hands outstretched to clasp and wring his neck.

The dogs sprang forward to defend their master.

'Hair!' the witch screamed. 'Tighten and strangle!'

Chaos broke loose! The hairs tightened around the beam, cutting it clean through and collapsing the wall of the hut; the dogs jumped on the witch, biting and yelping and the witch, wailing like a banshee, ran towards the door and vanished!

In the furore, the shepherd was knocked to the ground but he staggered to his feet to unlatch the door and set the dogs after her. Shaking like an aspen leaf, he waited for them to return but as time wore on he became very afraid. Then, the older collie returned with its tail tucked between its legs and blood smeared through its black and white coat. The young dog was killed by the witch.

Driven by a terrible feeling of dread for his family, the shepherd left his flock and rushed home to Glen Girnaig. On walking into his cottage his spirits lifted on finding his wife alive and well. However, when he opened his mouth to tell her of his ordeal she told him to tell her later. She was in a hurry to visit a neighbour who was so poorly the physican did not think she would survive the night.

Not wishing to let his kind-hearted wife out of his sight, nor for that matter remain alone by himself, he accompanied her out into the soaking evening.

When they went into the invalid's house, the shepherd cried out in alarm. Lying on the bed with a deathly pallor was the witch, her body fatally savaged by dogs.

The Urisk of Moness Burn

Before the noise and bustle of the Industrial Age drove them from the land, water sprites lived in almost every waterfall in Breadalbane. Tales of these faerie folk show some people describing them as goblins while others saw them as wee people with long flowing hair and often wearing bonnets.

Urisks were keen on food, very keen on food! They had a great love of fish and, in particular, milk. This may be why they made themselves useful to mortals by carrying out tasks like threshing their corn or other necessary jobs to be repaid in milk.

You would be mistaken, however, to assume urisks were always benign, good-humoured creatures. They were also well known for their naughty and downright destructive nature if they were upset. Unfortunately, being unpredictable was another aspect to their character, which sometimes made it hard to live with them as close neighbours.

This tale concerns the urisk they called Peallaidh (the Shaggy One). His full name was Peallaidh an Spuit and he lived among the rocks and waters of the Upper Fall of the Moness Burn, above Aberfeldy. His friend, a fellow urisk called Brunaidh an Easain (Broonie of the Smaller Fall), lived downstream on the lower waterfall.

Now, urisks are known for their longevity and it is claimed Aberfeldy was created by Peallaidh, the original Gaelic name being Obair Pheallaidh – The Work of Peallaidh.

Near Peallaidh's waterfall lived a farmer and his wife. Her turf-roofed cottage was always spick and span, her family well cared for and most days saw her humming away, preparing food over a glowing fire.

She was baking one day when Peallaidh came running in through her open door and snatched up her first batch of cooling bannocks.

The poor housewife was shocked and a little worried. If an urisk came into your home once, it would keep coming back. Out of the corner of her eye she watched the shaggy-haired little figure sitting at her table munching away at her scones. When the ones on the fire were ready, she tipped them on to the plate and hoped he would soon be full.

But no. As soon as Peallaidh's mouth was empty, with a savouring swallow and smack of his lips, he launched into one of the new ones. The woman stirred up more dough, deciding the only way to get rid of him was to fill this cheeky sprite until he could eat no more.

The woman's larder proved no match for the urisk's appetite. Soon, she feared he was going to eat all her food, leaving nothing for her family when they returned. She took longer than usual with the last batch, keeking over her shoulder from time to time to see when the urisk had finished the bannocks on the table.

'Here ye are,' she said pleasantly, using a cloth to pick up a new one, fresh from over the fire. She placed it straight into his hand.

With a screech of pain, Peallaidh dashed out the door. Shaking and blowing on his fingers, he fled through the ferns and birch trees to plunge his scalded fingers in the cold waters of Moness Burn.

At first, the woman was pleased to see him go and congratulated herself on getting rid of him. However, it was not long before she began chiding herself for hurting this affable wee sprite.

Up in his damp, dripping, trickling home under the torrents of the falls, Peallaidh was also mulling over his behaviour in a neighbour's home. Perhaps he had been a bit greedy? But the bannocks were delicious ... then again, had he not seen her use the very last of her flour? Would her family go hungry that night? He was not proud of himself.

The next day, the farmer's wife soothed her conscience by placing a cup of milk and a bannock by the waterfall. When she returned the following day, the cup was empty and the bannock gone. A lifelong pattern emerged when every once in a while she repeated this gift.

Peallaidh did not come to her kitchen again. However, soon after, a large dry patch on her husband's field became unexpectedly moist and fertile. On searching for the source of the new spring, they followed it back to the upper waterfall.

The farmer's wife was not the only one making amends.

The Wife of Beinn a' Ghlò

There were two men, friends, who were keen on hunting and set out together one fine winter day with plans to shoot themselves a twelve-pointer stag. They were told this Royal Stag had been seen with its herd on Beinn a' Ghlò, a range of forbidding mountains not far from the hunting lodge where they were staying.

They started off in high spirits, cracking jokes and striding along, their ghillie leading his highland pony behind them in readiness for bringing the beast off the hill. As the day wore on, clouds billowed up, sending snow flurries to powder a white dusting over the surrounding summits. The men pressed on.

By early afternoon the little hunting party had climbed a fair distance up the slopes, zig-zagging their way along sheep tracks lacing the rough terrain. It was steep and heavy going, causing them to pause to catch their breath more and more frequently, scanning the upper ground for any sign of the deer.

The ghillie did not like the look of the weather at all and pointed out the bank of snow clouds bearing in from the north.

'Let's see over the next rise,' one of the gentlemen decided, the puffs of his warm breath snatched away in the wind. 'If the herd's not there, we'll turn around.'

Within minutes, snowflakes spiralled down, settling and piling before a gust of wind whisked them up to join another floating wave. The ghillie lost sight of the huntsmen in the growing blizzard and after bellowing into the blurry white air, he gave up calling to them to come back. Fearing for his own safety, he concentrated on keeping his footing on the icy hill, turned the pony around and set it off in front of him to find a path for them both to reach the floor of the glen.

Further up the mountain, the two friends were in serious trouble. Weather changes fast on the mountains and before they knew it they were blinded by the white, whistling, whipping gusts swirling around them. Clutching onto each other, they inched their way along, bending double to keep their balance and praying their next step wouldn't plunge them into a ravine.

They could not tell east from west, down from up until they came upon a hut.

As soon as they were inside, they shut the door against the turmoil of the storm. It was dark in the hut but as their eyes became accustomed to it, they saw the red glow of flames and a figure crouched on the floor beside the hearth.

Neither man had ever seen such a strange creature before. It was an old woman, her scrawny body draped in a peculiar sleeveless shift showing her bare arms to be unnaturally elongated and thin. Long grey hair trailed over her shoulders with wisps obscuring the features of her face to give it the appearance of crumpled paper. She turned her head towards them, the loose skin beneath her chin creasing and puckering in folds. Her lips were moving, uttering a bold but tuneless song in unintelligible words.

Set deep in their shadowy sockets, her eyes focused on the men with a look that might terrify a coward.

The men were shivering with cold and stole closer to the fire, all the time expecting some movement or sound of aggression from the woman. None came.

With the passing of time and the warmth of the fire, the men's trepidation receded, to be replaced by hunger. They asked if she had any food.

Slowly she rose up, her long arms stretching towards them to present a fresh salmon.

'Little you thought I would give you your dinner today,' she said, a knowing smile rearranging the lines on her withered face. 'I can do more. It is I who blinded you with the storm and brought you here.'

The men spent the rest of the night in the hut and politely took their leave at first light. The sky was clear, the air sharp above the startling white ground.

The old woman watched them go, saying: 'I am the wife of Beinn a' Ghlò.'

Later that day, in the safety of the familiar, civilised drawing room of their hunting lodge and surrounded by their fellow guests, the men recounted their adventure. They could not decide whether the being they encountered was a mortal or a manifestation from another world, however both men were adamant in confirming the ordeal.

Serving staff overheard the account and it spread quickly among the locals, who were not surprised by the tale. Similar stories had been told for generations, affirming the presence of the Cailleach, or the guardian of the wildlife on the mountains, and many were comforted to know of her continuing presence.

DONALD OF THE CAVE

From the days of toddling beside their mothers, Donald and the little boy from the croft nearby would play together in the glen. As soon as they were old enough, they were expected to help with simple tasks, fetching and carrying around the home or feeding the animals. In the winter it was hard to find enough hours of daylight to be outside but in the summer, as soon as their chores were done, their parents would tell them to amuse themselves and 'mind not to get into any trouble!'

Donald was a lazy boy by nature. He disliked the daily drudgery of the hard work his father gave him: digging and planting the runrigs, milking the cow, churning butter or cutting and stacking peat. So, in long, warm evenings he would dash off to meet his friend to indulge in the far more pleasurable activities of guddling for trout, climbing trees or hunting for birds' nests.

By the time Donald was about twelve years old, the two young lads were venturing further afield up the hills and through neighbouring valleys. One day, they took the brae of Auchenruidh across the high moor and came upon a sheet of water known as Lochan na Carr. They were soon searching for pebbles at the water's edge to challenge each other in a skimming competition.

The evening was still and the sky a clear blue from one horizon to the other. The glassy-smooth surface of the loch reflected a perfect mirror image of the surrounding hills and trees. This sublime tranquillity was shattered by each stone they sent whirling and bouncing across the top of this upside-down image. Ever increasing circles of ripples emanated from where the stones touched the water, sending little waves to lap the shore.

Annoyed that his friend was managing to skim his stones further, sometimes with up to eighteen bounces, Donald took a long time finding one for his next attempt, allowing the water to return to its smooth surface.

'Look there now?' Donald cried. 'Ye see yon reflection of a tree on the water? There in front of us?'

'Aye,' his friend replied.

'Look behind, there is no tree!'

Their faces screwed up in confusion, the boys looked from the bank to the water and back again several times. Sure enough, the bank held only a few low aspens amid a mass of golden gorse, yet the flat mirror surface of the loch showed a tall Scots pine with sturdy branches.

'The tree should be right here!' Donald shouted with excitement, striding to the spot the trunk ought to be rising out of the ground. 'I'm going to find it and climb it because I think I can see it holds an osprey nest!'

Despite his friend being frightened by this inexplicable reflection, Donald kept searching. Waving his hands about in the air he suddenly felt the rough bark of a pine tree beneath his fingers. Keeping an eye on the reflection in the water below, he pulled himself nimbly up to the top branches and peered inside the nest. At first he was disappointed to find there were no eggs, just a stone lying in the middle. He picked it up.

'Can ye see me?' he called to the other lad.

'No! Where ha'e ye gone? I can hear ye but ye've vanished!'

'Then ye'll never see me again,' said Donald.

Donald's parents did not believe the neighbour's son when he returned home on his own. The boy cried with frustration, insisting Donald climbed a tree which was not there and found a special stone which made him disappear! What a wicked boy he was to tell such a lie, they chided him, fearful for Donald's safety. However, they soon began to suspect the tale was true.

With the Clach na Cur, 'Stone of Power', in his pocket, Donald was invisible and free to steal anything and everything he wanted, right from under the owner's nose. There would be no more back-breaking, palm-blistering work for him! That very evening the locals began reporting the loss of a pot of honey, a loaf vanishing from where it was left to cool, and a valuable horn-handled knife. There one minute, gone the next.

Soon, Donald realised he needed to find a safe place to conceal all his ill-gotten goods. Up on Glen Garry he found a secluded spot on Leacainn a' Bhainne and dug a large hole between rocks, deep underground, where he stashed his haul of gold, food and belongings. Across Perthshire there was barely a home, whether it be a croft or castle, which Donald did not visit and rob.

He found it terribly funny to move, unseen, around the minister's house, stealing his penknife and quills from the bureau while the good man was pacing about, just feet away, composing his sermon. It is believed Donald walked past a guard of soldiers when he stole a pair of golden candlesticks from Scone Palace.

On the last day of each month the Duke's tenants trekked to Blair Atholl to pay their rent at the Land Agent's window. Donald mingled with the queue, stealthily removing or emptying their money bags without them noticing. Weighed down with other men's hard earned gold and the rest of his pickings from the day, he went back up to Glen Garry and hid them away in his secret cave.

Searches were organised which saw shepherds and butchers, woodsmen and blacksmiths walking side by side with members of the gentry. They were at their wits' end and

determined to track down the invisible thief who, they soon
deduced, must have a place in which to hide the stolen property, yet no one could find Donald's cave.

Years went by and Donald grew up into a tall, fat man. His
invisibility fed his laziness, making his life reckless, irrespon-
sible and ruled by greed. From cones of sugar to chickens,
diamond brooches to coins, he had them all.

It was a dull, sleety day in winter when Donald wandered
onto Kindrochet land and spied a pig. He laughed to himself
and decided it would be amusing to own this grand boar.
Reaching past the farmer, he seized a length of rope hanging
on the pigsty, tied a noose around the pig's neck and hauled
it off.

The farmer gave chase, letting out a great shout which
brought his sons and wife running from the barn. They
could see him!

Three times he wriggled free from their grabbing hands
and stumbled on before being wrestled to the ground. He
released the pig and screamed for mercy, frantically clutching at his pocket but the pocket was empty. He had left the
Stone of Power behind in his cave.

Word of his capture spread rapidly and there was great rejoicing, but it was not enough to have Donald charged, they wanted their money and possessions returned.

He was sentenced to death at MacIntosh's Mod but offered the chance to save his life if he told them where his stash was hidden and handed over the Stone of Power.

Donald refused and went to his grave without ever divulging the location of the stone or his cave.

After Donald's execution, Thomas the Rhymer prophesied the stone would be discovered in the secret den and all the treasure stashed within it. It will be found, he said, by a red-haired woman with a dun coloured, wild-eyed dog while herding a white cow.

THE FAERIES OF KNOCK BARRIE

There was once a farmer, Ailbeart, who worked land up on the fertile slopes at Barrie, above the market town of Pitlochry. Ailbeart was a practical man, he toiled the earth and tended his animals but unlike his family and most of the local folk he was a steadfast disbeliever in faeries.

Late one spring afternoon before the land was greening, Lachlan, his neighbour from Tom Beithe, was going to meet a friend when he came across Ailbeart feeding his horse in a sheltered hollow. They passed a few words and the neighbour observed from the remnants of trampled hay and the muddy ground that this was a favoured place for the farmer to tether his horse.

Lachlan began to walk on, his eyes sparkling and his lips tugging into a smile. 'I'll be on ma way, then, Albie, but the day's drawing in, it will soon be dark. Are ye sure ye'll be all richt here, wi' the faeries of Knock Barrie?'

Ailbeart shook his head, 'Aye, very funny, there's no such thing!'

On arriving at his friend's house, a musician, Lachlan took out his own fiddle. The women-folk prepared some food and joined with their children dancing and clapping to the music in the bright firelight. It was a lively, noisy evening but throughout the jigs and banter, Lachlan was forming a plan. Before heading home, when all was quiet and the others were tucked into bed behind their drawn curtains, Lachlan and his friend shared a whisky beside the embers.

They agreed on a particular tune which they would both learn and practise over the following days. Then, with much muffled laughter, Lachlan made his way home under the light of the moon.

A week or so later, Ailbeart hammered in the last nail on the gate he was repairing, gathered some hay from a nearby haystack and trudged down to feed his horse. It was blustery on the hill and he was relieved to enter the calm shelter of the hollow. At first he thought the sound he heard must be from his own ears, still humming from the wind. Then there were distinct notes, tuneful, melodic.

He looked around and over his shoulder but there was no one in sight, yet he could hear music. His garron mare could hear it, pricking her ears as she munched her food. The music grew louder. It was the sweetest most harmonious tune Ailbeart had ever heard and he strained to tell where it came from. As he walked towards a pile of massive boulders on his left, the music grew louder and he hastened his pace, but just as he neared the first stones the tune died away …
and continued from behind him.

He swung round, glaring at the open ground, trying to gauge the source of this beautiful melody. The horse carried on eating, the wind rattled the winter bare saplings, a dog barked far away in the valley but above all these, pure and clear, musical notes sang in the air. Confused, he marched smartly towards the other side of the hollow where one large rock protruded from the heather. Sure enough, the music grew louder as he approached. It was moving into its jaunty, toe tapping refrain … then stopped … starting again immediately behind him, without missing a beat.

Back and forth the farmer went, back and forth the music played: continuously, smoothly, without the slightest falter to the course of the tune.

Suddenly, the farmer stopped.

Chills ran up his spine, making the hairs on his arms and up the back of his neck stand on end. This strange, ethereal music was unnatural: supernatural.

He fled up the hill. His heart was pounding with fear as he went scrambling and running across the hillside and into his house, where he threw himself on the bed.

After a good lie down, he felt no lasting damage from his peculiar experience. This was a relief to Lachlan and his fiddler friend, although they noticed he never again used the hollow as a place to keep his horse.

From that day onwards, there was no man, woman or child who could shake Ailbeart's absolute conviction that there *were* faeries on Knock Barrie.

SUNDANCING

He woke up and dressed silently, slipping his shift over his head then wrapping his plaid around him. His feet moved soundlessly across the packed-earth floor as he headed out into the night, the moon shining brightly overhead. He set off down the familiar track heading for Loch Ordie, his bare feet stepping firmly on the grassy path. He kept up his pace because he wanted to reach the loch before sunrise so he could see the sun dancing on the water.

Leaving the township of Tullymet behind, he soon reached the Allt Choire Bhuidhe (Burn of the Yellow Corrie), leaping over it easily at the crossing point before continuing on his way, the marshy ground squelching between his toes. On skirting round the rocky edge of Creag an Fhithich (Crag of the Ravens), a raven lifted off as he passed, calling out its disquiet at being disturbed. Then he dropped down the slope, swinging round into the glen that would lead him to the loch.

The sky was beginning to lighten so he quickened his steps, moving fast so as not to miss it. Soon, the winding path brought the water into view and after the last few twists and

turns he was at the loch's edge, the sky brightening rapidly. He moved round to his right to get the best view, found a sheltered spot in the lee of a great Scots Pine and settled down to watch.

He had a full day of calving ahead of him, but it had been worth the early start and hour's walk. He headed back with a smile on his face, whistling snatches of tunes as they came into his head. Moving easily along the path he rounded the base of Creag an Fhithich, and headed down towards the village. A movement caught his eye.

There, up on the crag, was a young woman kneeling down on the heather. As he watched, she reached her cupped hands out and put them in a small pool of water, her green dress mingling with the fresh young shoots. He smiled to himself; it must be one of the local lasses looking to see her future husband's face in the dew. An impish thought came to mind. While he was in no hurry to find himself a wife he was a one for tricks and having people on. What if the face she saw was his!

No sooner thought than done! He whistled to her loud and clear. She can't have heard as she didn't look up from what she was doing. He moved further round to get a clearer view and whistled again. Still no response. Irked by this, he was determined to get her attention so he moved down the path so she could see him clearly and whistled his loudest whistle. It worked. Her head jerked up and she looked straight at him.

He went cold. This was no local lassie. This was no less than the Queen of the Faeries. A very angry queen. Instantly he knew he was in trouble and his only hope was to cross the Allt Choire Bhuidhe as everyone knew faeries cannot cross running water.

He took to his heels and ran for his life, running faster than he'd ever run before. The burn wasn't far but the queen had her own ways to speed her. He heard her cry as she started her pursuit. His legs pounding, breath rasping, heart racing, he bolted towards the water knowing the faerie would be drawing ever closer. There was no time to get to the flat crossing point; he'd have to take his chance at the top where the burn carved a deep V in the land with steep sides and a steeper drop.

He stopped briefly at the edge to ready himself for the jump. Behind him he felt the air move as the queen closed in, her hands reaching out to grab him. He leapt desperately but she caught hold of his plaid. Stuck hard in her grip the plaid unfolded. He landed with a breath-losing thump on the opposite side. As he lay there stunned and breathless, the queen shredded his plaid into powder with her hooked, clawed hands and screamed in her anger.

'It's lucky yer oan the ither side of the burn; if I'd caught you, there wouldnae be a riddle in Tullymet that could riddle you and not let every scrap through.'

Left in only his shift, he scrambled to his feet and returned to the farm as quickly as his painful body could take him. Most people were up and working so he could quietly make his way to his quarters and don his work clothes before anyone saw him. He set about his tasks, moving slower than normal, his aching body protesting and his manner subdued, which was noted because he was one who liked to banter. There was a lot of work to do, it was a busy time of year but at the end of the day, when the sun had long set and they were all gathered round the fire, the story came tumbling out. Heads nodded.

'Aye,' said Tom the cooman. 'You were gey lucky, best keep yer een peeled as next time it may not go sae weel.'

As soon as he could, he found a position at another farm on the far side of Loch Ordie, far enough away not to see the Creag, and there he stayed, the man who outran the Queen of the Faeries.

WHAT NOT TO SAY TO A BROONIE

In the days long before the old A9, or the new A9, to get from Dunkeld to Pitlochry you followed a track over some gentle hills and through the woods. The track is still there today and used as a footpath.

The track was much travelled as people went to and from markets, visited friends and family and went further afield. As is common, alongside the track were farms, crofts and steadings. One such was Clochfoldich Farm which was a lucky farm because they had a broonie.

A broonie was a real gift to a hard-working farmer. They would come at night and do all the unfinished jobs. Dishes unwashed? A lovely, clean pile in the morning. Hole in the roof? Patched and watertight, and so on. Yes, having a broonie was invaluable but the farmer knew he had to look after the sprite as they could go, just as easily as they came. He knew the three golden rules of broonies:

Never offer a broonie clothes.

Never offer them food.

Never, ever, give them a name.

Well this broonie, as well as being helpful, had an unusual trait. It loved playing in the burn nearby and could oft be heard splashing and guddling around. As is the way with humans, it wasn't long before the farmer and his workers gave it names but the one that stuck was 'Puddlefoot'. Of course, they were very careful to only use it during daylight and in quiet voices among themselves.

One winter was particularly harsh. The snow banked up high above people's heads, sheep had to be dug out of deep drifts and people could get trapped for days by blizzarding snow. The farmer had been away to Perth to see to some business before the new year began and had battled his way up the road to Dunkeld. He stopped in a pub and greeted his many friends, enjoying a warming dram or two to get the chill from his bones.

'You'll be no setting aff in this?' his friend asked.

'Aye, I want my ain bed and tae celebrate Hogmanay at ma ain hoose,' he said. 'It's no' right to be awa' at the turning of the year. It's no far, I've done the worst of it.'

Well, none could disagree, so they waved him off on his cold, lonely journey. As the land got higher so did the snow. He knew it would be a tough journey. The snow driving into his eyes, head bowed to fend off the worst, tightly wrapped in his coat, he trudged on. He knew every inch of this path, even covered in deep snow, and after a while saw familiar markers that told him a warm bed and big dram were not far away. He brightened at the thought, imagining himself in dry clothes, feet by the fire and whisky in hand bringing in the New Year.

Suddenly, through the snow and wind he heard a crack and crash of ice breaking and the sound of splashing and guddling. He smiled to himself, 'Haha, even snow willnae stop Puddlefoot puddling!' he thought as he walked on. The splashing got louder until he was level with it and without thinking he called out 'Ho there Puddlefoot!'

There was a shriek and suddenly the farmer was confronted by an angry broonie.

'What did you call me? You gave me a name, did you?' and with that the broonie disappeared and was never seen at the farm again.

BLACK DOG OF DALGUISE

The young Pictish man stood proudly, his head held high, sword at his waist. He'd passed all the coming of age tasks and was now a warrior of the Nechtan tribe. His father and brothers before him had done the same and they greeted him now, not as a young boy but as a fighter, warrior, protector, hunter, farmer – a man.

His mother approached, carrying a squealing bundle and handed it to him. He looked down at the furry black shape and smiled. He'd helped train other men's war hounds, now it was his turn. He knew a well-trained hound would be invaluable, they would sense and flush prey, round up beasts, warn of approaching strangers and fight side by side in battle. A good war hound could save your life.

The young Nechtan quickly proved adept at training the dog, with the two becoming so close they could sense each other's moods and actions almost before they happened. This wasn't just a good war hound but a great one, one about which songs are sung and stories told. The tribe acknowledged the uncontested quality of the team and recognised this was something special. Man and dog were rarely apart.

The tribe was nomadic, like many Pictish people, moving to different pastures from summer to winter and back again; or up to high ground during floods or quiet places during time of threat. On the whole, they lived peacefully, tending their crops and beasts and living their lives.

As the season turned from summer to autumn the tribe packed up and prepared to move to their winter grounds. Moving slowly through familiar paths they traced their route through thick woodland of oak, ash and birch until suddenly one side opened onto a flat river plain. It was getting late, the light was going and a thick mist started to form above the wet ground, making it difficult to see who was ahead or behind. The normal chatter stopped as the eerie hush took effect. They walked on in silence. The war hound stopped and raised its head sniffing, tasting the air.

Suddenly, the ringing sound of a Carnyx, the Pictish war horn, ripped through the air. War cries erupted and the Garnat mac Domnach tribe came thundering through the trees, axes and swords drawn, dogs baying and the call of the Carnyx calling through the mist. The Nechtan tribe barely had time to ready themselves before the enemy was upon them. Desperate skirmishes broke out as people tried to distinguish friend from foe in the fog.

It quickly became a full-scale rammy with men, women, children and dogs on both sides fighting tooth and nail. The young warrior and his hound fought together as one, each anticipating each other's move, a team like no other. Man and dog were so intent on the foe in front of them, they failed to see a huge, grizzled man appear behind them.

When they realised, it was too late– the huge man swung his axe and the young warrior fell to the ground. His war hound let out a huge bay and leapt at the man, fastening his jaws and teeth around his throat, squeezing the breath out of him and crushing his windpipe. The man staggered back with the great black dog clenched around his neck and with his final breath he buried his axe in the dog's chest. The Garnat mac Domnach warrior and Nechtan war hound fell together on the ground, dead.

Later, when the battle was over and the mist cleared, both tribes searched the battleground for their dead and injured. The young warrior was found to be alive, grievously wounded but alive; he was gently removed from the field and handed into the care of the tribe's healer.

The Nechtan hound and Garnat mac Domnach warrior were also found, locked together in death and as they couldn't be separated they were left where they fell.

What happened to the young Nechtan warrior is not known but his loyal war hound seemed determined to find out.

Soon after the battle, people and tribes reported seeing a great shaggy black hound in the area. Sometimes it walked beside them, others said it sat and watched. Many tried to catch it because it was a fine beast, but none succeeded. A family who became lost in the thick mist told of a black dog who appeared and lead them through to safety. A Garnat mac Domnach man claimed to have been chased by a black hound he could not kill, no matter how he tried. The experience turned his hair and beard white.

Time passed, sightings grew rarer and then nothing was seen or heard of the dog for many, many years.

The land and people changed, the Picts disappeared and Scotland was formed under Kenneth McAlpine. A village grew at the site and was called Dalguise. Times and fashions changed and the Victorian era brought Scotland and big country houses into popularity. The grand Dalguise House was built for the Stewart family and later Stewartfield, the associated summer residence, up the hill.

Like the Picts, the family would winter in one house and spend the summer in the other. The area was soon alive with family, friends, visitors, ghillies, beaters and thriving kennels. Perhaps the influx of activity awoke the sleeping dog as reports of a large black hound were often made around both sites. The ghillies and kennel masters tried catching it – it would make a fine hunting dog – but to no avail.

Then, a strange thing was observed at the kennels. The kennels were full of their usual noise of barking, snapping and woofing when suddenly it stopped, like a light being switched off, and for a minute or so the kennels were still and quiet and all the dogs looked out in the same direction. They were watching something go by, an animal that demanded respect by the look of the dogs' behaviour. Even the feral estate cats that kept the mice down stopped and watched. This was repeated many times after.

With the popularity of Perthshire came the rise of the railway and work began on the highland line cleaving its way through the land from Perth to Inverness. The navvies laying the rails one day got an uneasy sensation and when they looked up, there was a great shaggy black dog watching them. It returned to the same spot every day, watching, but no matter what they did, offering food or trying to shoo it away, it returned.

The Highland Main Line opened and villages such as Luncarty, Stanley, Murthly, Dunkeld & Birnam, Dalguise, and Pitlochry all had their own stations, along with many others winding their way north. The stationmaster arrived and had a grand two-storey house at Dalguise beside the line. He brought with him a large hairy black dog, or so everyone thought, until they discovered he had a dainty tortoiseshell cat but no dog.

One day the engine was hurtling along towards Dalguise station when the driver saw a large black animal on the line ahead. He sounded the whistle but the animal did not move. In the end the driver slammed on the brakes, bringing the engine and carriages to a shaking halt. The fireman and stoker jumped out to move the beast but could find no sign of it when they walked up the rails. Then the stoker gave a loud cry and pointed to a thick branch wedged between the rails. It would have been hidden from the driver's sight until they were upon it and would almost certainly have derailed the train. A disaster was averted.

Years rolled by and once again the dog was seen less and less and then it wasn't seen for a very long time. The world changed and moved on. Dalguise House, where Beatrix Potter's family stayed for many summers, became an outdoor centre and the sister residence, Stewartfield, fell into ruins. After 100 years of service, the beautiful station at Dalguise fell victim to the Beeching cuts along with many others on the line and the station closed. In the 1970s the A9 was upgraded and its route altered, bypassing many villages and bringing it closer to Dalguise. Again, sightings of a great black creature were reported with many assuming it was part of the big cat phenomenon – an escaped panther perhaps. The estate kennels were abandoned but there was something there, a presence with glowing eyes.

One autumn, recently, a team was up from Glasgow, staying for a few weeks while they completed some complex repairs to one of the old buildings. One night the building's neighbours heard a loud hammering on their door. On answering, there was one of the young workmen, wide eyed and pale.

'Wolves!' he cried, shaking. 'Are there wolves here?'

The couple reassured him that there were no wolves left in Scotland, sat him down and gave him a dram.

'But there was a great, black, hairy shape with glowing green eyes!' he wailed.

'Ah,' they said, 'that will be the Black Dog of Dalguise.'

And so the dog continues to look for its lost master.

The Wild Man of Dunkeld

Dunkeld is a popular place for tourists and other visitors; walking and nature are major attractions with the river, The Hermitage and locally breeding ospreys as big draws. Much of the land either was, or still is, owned by the Duke of Atholl as part of the Atholl Estates but that wasn't always the case.

Many, many years ago the land around Dunkeld was owned by the Earl of Tullibardine. It happened that the Earl had only one child, a daughter. The girl was much loved by her family and by all the people around; his tenants, staff and others. Because of this she was allowed to wander wherever she liked, safe in the knowledge no harm would befall her and there would always be a watchful eye. She loved nothing more than walking round her father's lands, following the paths, roads and trackways. She especially enjoyed walking by the river and watching the wildlife through the seasons: the swifts and swallows darting around heralding spring, the wildflowers and younglings in the summer, the turning of the leaves and rutting of the stags in autumn and the flash of bright bushy tails in the winter as red squirrels danced past. She could sit for hours just watching and chatting to people around.

One day her father came to her and forbade her to leave the mansion house.

'But why father? I've never been stopped before,' she said.

'A great wild man, a savage, has been terrorising people in the area, jumping out and demanding food,' he told her. 'He's not hurt anyone, yet, but we can't be too sure. I want you to stay at home until he's caught. I don't imagine it will take long.'

So the young woman stayed at home, not a great hardship as it was a big house with large gardens so she still had places to walk. However, days passed and he wasn't caught; days turned into a week, then another. No matter what they did, the great wild man evaded the earl and his men. She grew restless, wanting to be out in her beloved land, so she took matters into her own hands. She declared that whoever caught the wild man she would marry.

Well, the hand of the Earl's only daughter was a great prize indeed and soon the countryside was alive with men, young and old, from near and far, trying to catch the wild man. They had no more success than the Earl.

The son of the ferryman decided to try; he'd spent his whole life in the area and knew it and its wildlife well. So, he thought and planned. Soon he set out looking for his quarry and after much careful searching he found him high in the crags. Instead of jumping out and attacking him, the young man followed him and did so for several days, trying to find a pattern or a place he could trap the man. After a while a pattern did emerge.

At the bottom of the crags of Craig a Barns, just beyond Polney Loch, a burn weaved its way down to the river. At one point the passage of water had carved out a hollow in the stone, like a natural bowl. The wild man would often visit, scooping water out of the bowl with his large hands. The young man knew what to do.

He went home and got a sack and in it put three bottles, he then returned to the hollow and hid in bushes and waited. Sure enough the wild man appeared and drank his fill as normal before heading off. As soon as he left, the young man sprang into action. He took some mud and branches from the surrounding area and dammed up the burn so it couldn't fill the bowl. He then reached into his bag and pulled out the first bottle, which was full of an amber-coloured liquid; removing the stopper, he poured the whole contents into the bowl. When it was empty, he took out another bottle of the same amber-coloured liquid and emptied that too. Finally he reached in again and took out the third bottle – a shorter, wider one. Opening it, he scooped out the contents, adding a thick straw-coloured liquid and then stirred it around so it mixed well.

He returned to his hiding place and waited. Sure enough the great wild man appeared and knelt by the bowl and cupped his hands to drink the water. After the first taste, he threw himself onto the ground with his face in the bowl where he sooked up the mixture in huge drafts until it was gone. He then licked the sides of the bowl and, when he was sure he had got every last bit, he went to stand up. His legs wobbled underneath and he toppled over, landing on his back, fast asleep and snoring loudly.

The young man jumped out from where he was sitting and quickly bound his captive's wrists and ankles so he couldn't move. He then dashed off to tell the Earl.

The Earl and his men came quickly and saw the ferryman's son had achieved what no one else had managed.

The daughter kept her word and she and the young man were married. Some say they were already sweethearts and this was a ploy to let them marry across the social divide.

The wild man was taken to a remote place far from Dunkeld where he could live peaceably, bothering no one and being bothered by no one. Every week the villagers would leave food for him, much like a hermit might live in a hermitage.

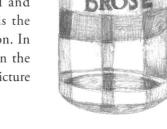

Much later on, the Tullibardine and Atholls intermarried and the Earl of Tullibardine is the title of the duke's eldest son. In the Atholl coat of arms, in the bottom left quadrant is a picture of a wild man.

But what of the brew that defeated the wild man? Well, it became known as an elixir for all ills, credited with bringing people back from the brink of death. It is still drunk in Dunkeld and goes by the name of Athole Brose.

IN THE FOOTHILLS OF SCHIEHALLION

Schiehallion towers over Rannoch Moor, its pointed peak instantly recognisable at a distance. With its three false summits and rocky top, it can be a frustrating walk that rewards with far-reaching views and a hill well climbed. It has a unique place in history, as Nevil Maskelyne used it to calculate the mean density of the Earth, but it is far better known by its other name – Hill of the Faeries.

Two brothers lived their whole lives in the shadow of the hill, working the land, seeing it through the seasons and the many changes in practice, politics and techniques that happened over time. Both men in their day were tall, strong and broad shouldered, with thick dark hair and dark eyes the colour of the land itself. As time went on, as oft happens to people who work the land, their backs became crooked until both were humpity backed, their heads drooping lower than their shoulders and a great hump rising from between their shoulder blades.

While the brothers were much alike in looks down to their humps they couldn't be more different as people. One brother, the younger, always had a cheery word and would be the first to help anyone, finding the last few coins in his pocket and a smile that warmed everyone. The older brother was constantly crabbit, with never a good word to say, and on being asked to help would say if anyone needed help it was him. Having spent their lives working around Schiehallion, after they retired they both spent their days walking the land they loved and knew every inch. They were a familiar sight with their thick walking sticks fashioned from birch with handles carved from horn, by their own hands, one with a happy wave and a smile and one with a grimace.

One day the younger brother was out walking, as usual, when he came across a path he hadn't seen before. He thought he knew this area like the back of his hand so was puzzled. He followed the rough track along the base of the hill leading up and down the bumpy track. As he walked, he began to catch a sense of music and song and, as he went on, the music got louder and words of the song became clearer until he reached a mound where it was at its loudest.

He stopped and listened, the words of the song clearly reaching him. 'Monday, Tuesday, Monday, Tuesday.' He had never heard anything so sweet and beautiful and so he slowly pulled himself to the top of the mound and peered over. There, beneath him, was a circle of faeries, the wee folk, playing instruments and singing their song, 'Monday, Tuesday, Monday, Tuesday.'

The brother was transfixed but he couldn't help himself and sang out 'Wednesday, Thursday.'

The faeries stopped and suddenly a faerie, taller than the rest, appeared in front of him. The brother froze, he knew the power of the faeries and what could happen if they were annoyed.

'What were those words?' asked the King of the Faeries.

'Er …' stuttered the brother, 'I just thought it was the most beautiful thing I'd ever heard and wanted to help continue the song.'

The King looked at the brother with his bright eyes and a steady gaze and moved his head, perhaps in a small nod.

The brother took this as a sign to continue: 'I thought I would add the next words – Wednesday, Thursday.'

'Come with me,' said the King and immediately the brother was surrounded by faeries helping him down the mound into the circle below. 'Please teach us those words.'

So, the brother sat with the faeries and taught them the new words and spent the rest of the day singing and talking and laughing with them until it began to grow dark.

'Ach, I should be off to my bed. Thank you for your hospitality and company, I've fair enjoyed it.'

'Thank you for our new words,' they sang out. The King stood before him, in his hand a clinking bag. 'Please take this with our thanks.'

'No, no,' said the brother. 'Sharing the words and enjoying your company is enough thanks.'

As he clambered ungainly to his feet, he groaned and rubbed his back where he had grown stiff and sore from sitting so long, his chest tight from the weight of the hump pressing down. The King watched and dropped his head, perhaps in a small nod. The brother hobbled off towards the path, pausing to turn and wave, but the faeries had gone. He wearily made his way home, his head full of song, and fell into bed face first, fully clothed into an exhausted sleep.

The next morning, he was woken by the sun streaming in and he felt awake and alert. He swung his legs to the edge of the bed ready to lever himself upright but as he did so, he felt different. As usual he stretched his arms and legs to start the day but this morning his arms, which could barely go past his shoulders, kept going until they were above his head. He hadn't been able to do that in years. He went to stand up and, as he did so, he found he could stand taller and taller until, for the first time in many a year, he could stand straight up.

His humph had gone. He walked quickly over to the mirror to check but they had all been hung at a lower level for him to use when he was crookit backed. He lifted the mirror off the wall and held it up and, sure enough, the humph was gone.

It was not long before the story of the brother's miraculous transformation spread through the glen and reached his elder brother. 'What?' he roared and bustled off to see for himself. Sure enough his younger brother was standing straight, as he was when a younger man, not a hint of a crook.

'What? How did you lose your humph?' he demanded, and so his brother told him the story of the unknown path, the faeries and the song.

At first light the elder brother hustled off, walking round and round the base, up and down the hill day after day with no result. Until suddenly, one day, he came to a path he'd never seen before and, as quickly as he could, he hobbled along faster and faster and soon song and music appeared in the air, getting louder and louder the closer he got.

When he reached the mound, he could hear 'Monday, Tuesday, Wednesday, Thursday, Monday, Tuesday, Wednesday, Thursday.'

'FRIDAY!' he bawled out and limped down to where the faeries were sitting speechless at this appearance. 'Right, I've finished your song for you, now give me my reward! Do something with my back and a bag of your gold will be welcome.'

The King of the Faeries stood up, looked at the older brother and dropped his head, perhaps in a small nod. 'Here is the bag of gold you wanted,' he said, reaching into his coat. 'And we will do something about your back.'

'Good,' said the brother, almost snatching the bag before rushing off without a backward glance or a word of thanks.

He hurried home and fell into a deep sleep, face first, fully clothed and clutching the bag. When he woke up the next morning he felt different. His chest was unbearably sore and his shoulders ached. He went to swing his legs over the edge of the bed but found it difficult to move. Slowly, he managed to stretch his legs and then tried to stand up, but his back was so heavy he was folded double with his head practically on his knees. He reached a hand to feel his back but could barely get past his waist so he shuffled awkwardly over to the mirror. Squinting into it, he could see his back.

Where there was once one humph, there were now two! The bag of gold lay on the floor, empty; as faerie gold dissolves at first light.

His younger brother soon heard of his plight.

'Brother,' he said, 'you shouldn't have upset the faeries. Find them, apologise, and see if they will undo their work, for only they can.'

And so the elder brother, slowly, painfully, shuffled off to walk the land of Schiehallion, hill of the faeries, to find the King. He walked and walked and some say he is still there today, looking for the path to the faeries to beg their forgiveness. If you visit Schiehallion, perhaps you'll see him and if you're lucky enough to meet the faeries, remember to be polite.

GLOSSARY

apairt – apart
bairn – child
biggit – built
blether – to chat
broonie – one of the faerie or 'ither' folk, helps round the
  house. Good to have.
chap – knock (chapped the door, knocked at the door)
clarsach – a small or knee harp
cooried – snuggled
drookit – soaked
een – eyes
ghillie – gamekeeper
gloaming – twilight
humph – hump or crooked back
jaikits – jackets
kist – a chest or trunk
lochan – a small loch or lake
mair – more
nicht – night

pibroch – a form of music for the Scottish bagpipes involving elaborate variations on a theme

rammy – pitched battle

runrig – narrow strips of land

sheiling – a hut used by those tending animals on high ground

sicht – seen

stooking the sheafs – stacking the wheat sheaves

theekit – thatched

thocht – thought

urisk – water sprite, similar to a broonie

Scottish Storytelling Forum

The Scottish Storytelling Centre is delighted to be associated with the *Folk Tales* series developed by The History Press. Its talented storytellers continue the Scottish tradition, revealing the regional riches of Scotland in these volumes. These include the different environments, languages and cultures encompassed in our big wee country. The Scottish Storytelling Centre provides a base and communications point for the national storytelling network, along with national networks for Traditional Music and Song and Traditions of Dance, all under the umbrella of TRACS (Traditional Arts and Culture Scotland). See www.scottishstorytellingcentre.co.uk for further information. The Traditional Arts community of Scotland is also delighted to be working with all the nations and regions of Great Britain and Ireland through the *Folk Tales* series.